I0764654

x3

Science Fiction

Other books by Gary A. Braunbeck

Collections:

Things Left Behind

Escaping Purgatory: Fables in Words and Pictures (co-authored with Alan M. Clark)

Sorties, Cathexes, and Personal Effects

Graveyard People: The Collected Cedar Hill Stories, Volume 1

From Beneath These Fields Of Blood

A Little Orange Book of Odd Stories

x3

Novels:

The Indifference of Heaven

In Hollow Houses

This Flesh Unknown

Isaac Asimov's I-BOTS: Time Was (co-written with Steve Perry)

Non-Fiction:

Fear In A Handful Of Dust: Horror As AWay Of Life

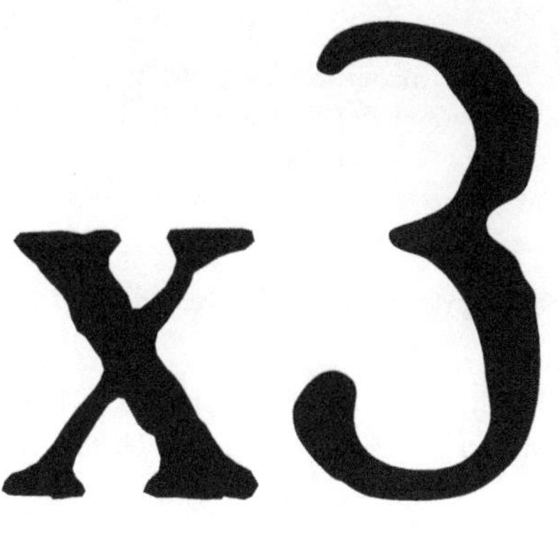

Science Fiction

GARY A. BRAUNBECK

BETANCOURT
& COMPANY
Doylestown, Pennsylvania

A Betancourt & Company Original.
Copyright © 2004 Gary A. Braunbeck.
All rights reserved.

Cover art copyright © 2004 by Ronald Horsley.

"One Brown Mouse" originally appeared in *Alien Abductions*, edited by Martin H. Greenberg and John Helfers, DAW Books, 1999.

"At Eternity's Gate" originally appeared in *A Dangerous Magic*, edited by Denise Little, DAW Books, 1998.

"Palimpsest Day" originally appeared in *Past Imperfect*, edited by Martin H. Greenberg and Larry Segriff, DAW Books, 2001.

It should be noted here that the versions of the stories which appear in *x3* have been specifically revised for this collection, and should be considered the preferred text.

x3
An original publication of
Betancourt & Company, Publishers
P.O. Box 301
Holicong, PA 18928-0301
www.wildsidepress.com

FIRST EDITION

Dedication

To Ray Bradbury, Charles Beaumont, William F. Nolan, Dan Simmons, Harlan Ellison, Jack Finney, Theodore Sturgeon, Robert Heinlein, Richard Matheson, and Rod Serling, in whose collective shadow I happily and humbly walk.

Contents

Twenty-Two Fathoms Down with Gary Braunbeck

by Brian A. Hopkins

"Man has places in his heart that do not exist, and into them enters suffering in order that they may have existence."

– Leon Bloy (1846–1917)

The above is one of several quotes by Leon Bloy that I've collected over the years. All writers, you see, collect such things – aphorisms, epigrams, snippets of poetry and such – because we are, in effect, at least the good writers amongst us, very clever thieves. I'm a thief. Gary Braunbeck is a thief. Writing in a total vacuum, purely from internal knowledge and imagination, will only carry you so far. Sooner or later, a writer who's any good, a writer who's here to stay, has to go in search of ideas and data external to himself, has to replenish and add new ingredients to the bubbling cauldron of his muse. What's interesting is that Gary and I have apparently been stealing from some of the same sources over the years. It's a wonder we haven't started stealing from each other!

I first used the Bloy quote as the epigram to a poem ("That They May Have Existence," 1996) and had always intended to use it with a story, until I saw that Gary had already done so ("Matters of Family," 1989). I've noticed other things in his work, concepts and ideas and descriptions where I've had to nod my head and say, "Ayup, I know what Gary was reading at the time." I even gigged him on it once, citing a paragraph from one of his short stories and sending him an email which simply read, "So, I'm not the only one who has read Lewis Thomas's *Lives of a Cell . . .*" (If *you* haven't, shame on you!)

So Gary and I are both thieves. And we're both very well read. Both good-looking chaps (if I do say so myself) born about the same time, influenced by the same television shows, music, teenage angst, and so on. I also like to think we're both damn good writers, though I think he might be a wee bit better. (Here's where Gary says, "No, *you're* the better writer." And I say, "No, *you* are!" And we go back and forth like that for hours until we finally decide neither one of us really knows much about anything.) There is, however, a fundamental difference in the process by which we both write, and to illustrate that difference, I'm going to return to the Bloy quote.

Leon Bloy was a remarkable but little known French writer, the author of several autobiographical novels *(Le Désespéré, La Femme Pauvre, Salut par les Juifs)* and *L'Exegese des Lieux Communs,* which examines bourgeois wisdom and proposes that life is worth living in and of itself (as opposed to merely existing as some transitional stage to the greater glory of Heaven, which is what the Catholic Church at that time would have had us believe). Bloy lived in poor quarters in the Montmarte in the shadow of the Basilique du Sacré Coeur. He preached spiritual revival through suffering and poverty. He was known for vituperative attacks on religious conformism, denunciations of cruelty and injustice, and bitter portraits of his life and friends. Reading his work, you might come away thinking that he was one gloomy goddamn bastard – and he probably was. But he used it to good effect.

With me so far? Good. File that away for the moment. Next I'm going to let you in on a secret. I hate introductions to short story collections. More to the point, I hate introductions that go on about the stories you're about to read, either telling you what they're all about (often spoiling them), or explaining why you should want to read them (if I bought the damn book, I must have wanted to read the stories, right?), or telling me how I'm supposed to feel after I read them (I'll figure that out on my own, thank you very much!). Having lately been asked to write a number of introductions for various short story collections and anthologies, I've hit upon my own technique for not boring the reader (who I imagine is no different than me and would just as soon skip the introduction and jump straight to the stories). I simply slip in an interesting story of my own. Not only is it more entertaining, I think, than reading about the book you've already bought, but it's a neat way for me to get something out of this whole introduction writing shtick! I mean, you don't think they're actually paying me for this, do you? But never fear, in the end, with some daring prestidigitation, I intend to tie all these loose threads together. Bear with me just a wee bit longer.

Having long been enchanted by the sea, I've recently taken up scuba diving. As with most of my passions, I dived in (if you'll pardon the pun) with both feet, spending four grand or so on equipment and another four or five grand on a big adventure trip to Costa Rica (which I'm preparing for as I write this introduction). Being an anal-retentive research addict, I've been reading a lot about diving and the history of scuba, uncovering all sorts of really cool information and stories (all of which is merrily bubbling away in that cauldron I mentioned). What I want to share with you here is the little known story of John Day.

John Day, an 18th century carpenter from Suffolk, England, intended to prove that he could survive for 24 hours underwater in a wooden diving chamber that he designed and built. Day spent three months building the contraption, using the best carpentry and joinery skills of the time. There is some record of preliminary testing, but accounts are sketchy. According to Richard Compton-Hall (*The Submarine Pioneers,* Sutton Publishing), "Some accounts speak of him deliberately sinking to a depth of 30 feet . . . and surfacing unharmed 24 hours later; but the version which has him simply allowing the tide to cover and uncover the beached contrivance is more credible."

When the submersible was ready, Day went in search of a backer. Christopher Blake, a wealthy gentleman from London, financed the operation, spending £340 on an old 50 ton sloop called the *Maria.* Day's chamber, a 12 foot long box containing some 75 hogsheads of air, was fixed to the *Maria's* deck by a complex system of struts and ropes. On a sunny afternoon – June 20, 1774 to be precise – a barge towed the *Maria* to a spot just north of Drake's Island in the middle of Plymouth Sound, where the depth was known to be 22 fathoms (130 feet). The sloop was to be sunk by means of two holes drilled in her hull. After a day and a night on the seabed, Day was to return to the surface by releasing the ties anchoring his chamber to the deck.

Without fanfare or send-off, Day removed his coat, telling the barge captain that it would be too warm inside the box. Then, with what an observer later called "great composure and confident in his enterprise," Day closed the hatch. The wooden plugs were removed from the holes in the *Maria,* and her stone ballast settled her gently into the sea. A quarter of an hour later, ominous bubbles were seen on the surface.

But John Day was never seen again.

A glimpse at Day's plans for his submersible reveal that few men have ever worked so long and hard at constructing their own coffin. Day had even rigged the box with three colored buoys with which he might signal his condition to the barge waiting above. White indicated that he was "very well." Red that he was "indifferent." And black signified "very ill." None of the buoys ever appeared on the surface.

A report published a year later (*Philosophical Dissertation on the Diving Vessel Projected by Mr. Day, and Sunk in Plymouth Sound,* N.D. Falck) concludes that Day must have been "thunderstruck with cold at the end of his rapid descent; so as to exhaust all vilifying warmth." Dressed lightly, Day would have been quickly chilled – if we assume he sank smoothly to the seabed and survived on the air contained in his box. At 22 fathoms, the sea temperature would have been no more than 54 degrees Fahrenheit. (Having recently dived in a Texas quarry where the water temperature was 57 degrees, I can assure you that, even while wearing 8 millimeters of high-tech neoprene, 45 minutes underwater is enough to chill an active diver, let alone someone sitting on the floor of a box.) Day would have suffered hypothermia: violent shivering, muscle spasms, rigidity, mental dissolution, and the slow but certain stalling of his heart. Undergoing these symptoms, it would have been difficult for him to release the complicated bolts securing his box to the deck of the *Maria.*

More likely, however, is that a catastrophic failure of the box's integrity occurred, leading to implosion and a quick death by drowning. At that depth, pressure is five times what is experienced on the surface. Any flaw, any loose seam or inferior joint, would have immediately flooded the box.

So there's your story . . . but what does all this mean: Leon Bloy's quote; John Day's box; Gary Braunbeck and myself?

When I write, I invite – nay, *long for* – distractions. I'm easily pulled away from the computer. Television programs, books, email, a walk through my woods, a willy-nilly Google-driven Internet excursion, *anything* of even the remotest interest is liable to sidetrack me. It's how I work. It's how I find elements to lend depth to what I write. But Gary . . . Gary closes himself off, shuts down – even to the detriment of his own health (see the author's notes in his collection, *Sorties, Cathexes, and Personal Effects,* if you doubt me). It's the only way he can create. He's like John Day, sinking into an abyss of his own creation, a dark cavern of isolation whose destination is some new region of the human heart. At the core of any Braunbeck story, you see, is humanity: what it means to be human, to live and suffer and explore Bloy's innerspace.

What you'll find in this book are three stories, "Palimpsest Day," "At Eternity's Gate," and "One Brown Mouse." The publisher would have you believe they're science fiction or horror or whatever, but they are quite simply Braunbeck Stories, like nothing else you'll ever read. He created them by going where you and I perhaps cannot.

So, the bad thing is that Gary's down there, 22 fathoms deep in his own personally designed isolation chamber, but the good news is that he's sending up signal flags, letting the rest of us know about the deep dark warrens he's uncovered in the human heart. I, for one, can't thank him enough.

Brian A. Hopkins
At Road's End, Oklahoma City
May 2003

Preface

A Few Stolen Moments of Your Time, Please

In his benchmark collection *The Third Level* (one of the few books that can justifiably be referred to as a "forgotten classic"), the late Jack Finney penned what I consider to be two of the finest time-travel stories ever written: "Such Interesting Neighbors" (which suffered an abysmal, ham-fisted adaptation on NBC's *Amazing Stories,* I'm sad to say) and "There Is a Tide . . ." Both stories deal with the age-old subject of travelers from, respectively, the future and the past making their presence known to, and having a concrete effect on, characters in the present.

Reads like fairly basic "Everybody-Knows-This" SF-101 stuff as I insufficiently describe them above, but these two stories – as can be said for every piece in that remarkable collection – never do exactly what you're expecting of them. Suffice to say that I, a life-long reader of science fiction, found myself not only surprised and moved by these stories, but left with a you-should-pardon-the-expression sense of wonder, something that happens all too rarely for me as a reader. Finney blindsided me with an expert (and, from a writer's standpoint, envy-inducing) sleight-of-hand whose "How-In-The-Hell-Did-He-*Do*-That?" equation I still, some fifteen years and easily thrice as many readings after the fact, cannot figure out. He resorts to no gimmicks, no cheap trickery, and steadfastly avoids getting tangled up in the old and wheezing Gordian knot of the *(yawn)* time-travel paradox – a theme that should have been abandoned by all intelligent writers after the publication of Robert Heinlein's "By His Bootstraps," as far as I'm concerned.

(Long parenthetical pause here, so get comfy: Consider, if you will, the first two *Terminator* movies if you need an example of how the "paradox" element cannot only shoot a story in the foot, but shove the business-end of a double-barrel shotgun in its mouth and trip both hammers: At somewhere around the ninety-minute mark of *Terminator 2,* Ah-nald confronts the wonderful Joe Morton, here playing Miles Dyson, the man responsible for the creation of the T-100 (or, technically, if you want to pick nits, the warm and fuzzy T-101 Arnie plays in the sequel). Arnie, in a blatantly-stated effort to stop his own future creation, peels back the synthetic skin on his arm to show Morton what he is, what Morton must never create. With me so far? Good. Now, apply what you know from decades of reading exemplary time-travel-paradox stories to that moment; not only should the movie have logically – and I'm being charitable by employing that word – ended right then and there, but since the T-100 (or T-101, whatever, like it matters or James Cameron gives a shit) would never have been created, the events depicted in *The Terminator* would not have occurred in the first place and we would have been spared four hours and twenty-seven minutes being sucked forever from our lives. If James "Everything-I-Do-Is-Brilliant-And-Don't-You-Forget-It" Cameron would have left things as they stood at the end of the first movie (which I thoroughly enjoyed), that would have been fine; it was *more* than fine, was, in fact, brilliant, when Harlan Ellison originally penned the story as "Soldier" on the classic *Outer Limits.*

(You're getting the idea, despite the subtlety of my presentation, aren't you? The time-travel-paradox can burn your ass seven ways from Sunday; in the case of *Terminator 2,* it not only destroyed the storyline by ignoring the rules so painstakingly established in the first movie, it insulted viewers' intelligence by straining all credibility and limping along for *another full hour* before reaching its ludicrous, self-defeating conclusion. And we're about to see a *third,* God help us, installment this summer of a series that, had it followed its own internal logic, should never have been made to begin with. Cameron should have realized that *no one* dumb enough and arrogant enough to try and make an Ellison story their bitch walks away unscathed. End of parenthetical rant.)

Don't misunderstand; I love good time-travel stories, regardless of the author's individual take on the theme, but I have far too much respect for science fiction to think this type of story can be done easily or its subject matter approached lightly; if I *were* foolish enough to think it easy, I'd have only to read the two Finney stories mentioned earlier to put me in my place. If that didn't do the trick, then they, combined with any of the following, would humble me no end: "12:01" by Richard Lupoff (adapted as a magnificent short film, then as the Bill Murray vehicle *Groundhog Day)*; "Yesterday Was Monday" by Theodore Sturgeon; "Jeffty Is

Five" and "Paladin of the Lost Hour" by Harlan Ellison (as well as the *Outer Limits* episodes "Soldier" and "Demon With A Glass Hand"); "A Sound Like Thunder" and "Forever and the Earth" by Ray Bradbury; "10^{16} to 1" by James Patrick Kelly; the afore-mentioned "By His Bootstraps," as well as "The Unpleasant Profession of Jonathan Hoag" by Robert Heinlein; *Portrait of Jenny* by Robert Nathan (the uncontested granddaddy of time-slip stories); *Lincoln's Dreams* by Connie Willis; Richard Matheson's elegant, elegiac *Bid Time Return*; even such plot-holed classics as H.G. Wells's *The Time Machine* and Edward Bellamy's *Looking Backward* would give me more than a little pause, simply because they, despite their flaws (which are far from fatal), established the template.

There are a handful of other stories and novels that I feel stand as a testament to what a good time-travel story can do in the hands of a writer whose commitment to bettering their craft (and, as a result, the field of science fiction) is unwavering, but I think the above list should erase any lingering doubts you may have as to my respect for, and at-least-journeyman knowledge of, this particular staple of the field.

In the seventeen years that have elapsed in a blink since I made my first professional short story sale to Alan Rodgers at *Twilight Zone's* sister magazine, *Night Cry*, I have published somewhere in the neighborhood of two hundred stories, the majority of them in the field of horror and dark fantasy (which are *not* the same thing, thank you very much), and while I'm honored to number myself among the members of the H/DF community, I tend to think of myself as more of a cross-genre writer in the Fabulist tradition of Gabriel Garcia Marquez, William Kotzwinkle, and Jack Cady, to name but three (and, no, I'm not saying that my work can rightfully take its place beside theirs – I'm not quite *that* conceited . . . or stupid – only that I strive to make my stories as honest, unpretentious, and unique as may befit minor inclusion in that noble area of storytelling.

I offer that as something of an olive branch because, of all the genres (pardon that word) that seem to be perpetually at bitter odds with one another, horror and science fiction to my eyes remain locked in the literary equivalent of the Hatfield and McCoy Feud. Don't ask me why, I've never understood this sometimes hell-bent Screw-'Em Jones the two fields have on for one another, especially vicious at the far ends of the spectrum (hard science fiction and extreme horror). Hard science fiction writers think horror authors suffer a self-afflicted case of arrested literary adolescence and wouldn't recognize a good idea if it announced itself with an Inspiration Enema, while horror writers think hard science fiction authors are geeky, virginal, intellectual snobs who still live in Mom & Dad's basement and wouldn't know an honest emotion if it sprouted fangs and bit them in the Happy Sacks.

Is it any wonder that you almost never see a cross-genre horror story in the ToC of Dozois's *The Year's Best Science Fiction,* or that anything that even remotely smacks of science fiction rarely finds its way onto the Horror Writers Association's Bram Stoker Award ballot?

I would not dare to speak on behalf on the science fiction community, but as a very active member of the H/DF community I feel right in saying that, believe it or not, we respect what you do, despite protestations otherwise by certain individual members of the horror field.

That being said, as a horror writer I would like to add the following request to the science fiction community at large: *Please* stop basing your opinions of horror on the *tsunami* of insipid, badly-written, half-assed, sloppy, ill-conceived, intellectually offensive, laughably-executed, and all-around not very good crap-for-crap crop of paperbacks that glutted the market in the 80s; it's 2003 as I write this, and the horror field has matured considerably; its writers and editors are much more well-read than they were twenty years ago, are taking more chances, and are, overall, striving to achieve more in their fiction than just a good shudder, jump, or gross-out; some of the work being produced in the field today is darn-near *literary* . . . not to mention literate. Who'd a thunk it possible?

This is not intended as an apology; I have no patience for apologists in any field of writing. It's a simple statement of facts as I see them . . . which, admittedly, might be a tad skewed, but I hope not ill-informed.

Now that I've dug myself so deep into a hole I can see Arne Saknussemm's skeletal hand starting to emerge between my feet, I nervously offer you *x3,* my first collection of science fiction stories – specifically, time-travel stories.

Permit me to repeat something I said earlier: I have far too much respect for science fiction to think this type of story can be done easily or its subject matter approached lightly. As I wrote each of the trio of tales you're about to encounter, my admiration for writers of science fiction increased exponentially with each story's completion. Because I so love science fiction and have read it for most of my life, I hope that my awareness (notice I didn't say "knowledge?") of what has been done before with this particular theme informed my various takes with an at-least-partially fresh perspective. You will not find any "paradox" elements in these three stories simply because A) I think it's been done to death, and too often badly (see long *Terminator*

2 rant earlier) and, B) I readily admit that I am neither clever enough nor smart enough to find a new approach to that element without eventually succumbing to cliché.

In short, I offer these stories as one who, though he writes far outside the science fiction field and is occasionally permitted the play in SF's back yard, nonetheless has a deep and abiding respect for its traditions. I was – and remain – quite proud of these stories, and hope that you find them worth a few stolen moments of your reading time.

– Gary A. Braunbeck
Columbus, Ohio
May 2, 2003

One Brown Mouse

"But Mousie, thou art no thy-lane,
In proving that foresight may be vain:
The best laid schemes o' Mice an' Men
Gang aft agley,
An' lea'e us naught but grief an' pain,
For promis'd joy!"

– Robert Burns

The thing which most bothered Levon about the other members of the grief support group – besides their voices seeming too loud because he was starting to get one of his corkscrew headaches – was not so much that they looked like prisoners awaiting the hour of their execution, but that every last one of them had the air of a *falsely-accused* prisoner, one who'd resigned him- or herself to dying for a crime they knew they did not commit – *'Tis a far, far better thing I do now than I have ever done before* and other such urp-inducing romantic fal-de-ral.

He sat, as always, slightly off to the side, hands fused into one ten-fingered white-knuckled fist pressed against his lap, trying to ignore the throbbing of his leg in its uncomfortable metal brace and praying to the ever-loving God whose grace and love had seen fit to put him in this position: *Don't let them make me talk, don't let them make me say her name . . . oh, yeah – since I've got your attention – if you're there at all – it'd be great if I didn't have the damned eyes dream again tonight, thanks so much: those big black almond-shaped bastards give me the willies.*

Of all the nights he'd not wanted to be here, this evening took the blue ribbon.

Which actually made it no different from any other evening that involved his being around other people; he was turning into an award-caliber anti-socialite.

He closed his eyes and pulled in a deep breath that immediately seared his lungs and made him hack, forcing tears from his eyes . . . then he realized he'd forgotten about the cigarette in his mouth. He yanked out the cancer stick and crushed it out on the floor, wiped the choke-tears from his cheeks, slammed a fist against his chest to jump start his dignity, and looked up to see the other group members staring at him. Jenny Collins, who'd lost her husband to a brain tumor eleven months ago, and who'd been talking about a man at work who recently asked her out to dinner, looked both annoyed and relieved that Levon had wrenched the group's attention away from her.

"You okay, Levon?" asked Dr. Hunter, the therapist in charge of the group. As usual, Hunter was playing with his "think-coin" (Levon's private term for the thing), one side of it red, the other green, flip/twirling it through the fingers of his hand – an old magician's dexterity exercise – yet despite this nearly-perpetual activity, his attention never swayed from what was happening with the group.

Hunter's stare grew concerned as the silence stretched. "*Levon?*"

Don't speak, Levon ordered himself; *if you speak, someone's bound to try to get you to go on. That's called communication, and we'll be having none of that.*

He nodded his head vigorously and offered a quick, embarrassed wave. Oops, silly me, sorry.

The drilling pain in the center of his skull – ever-present, it seemed, since he'd been released from the hospital – receded to the back, ebbing ever so slightly, but leaving just enough of a throb in its wake to remind him that it was still there and probably always would be.

Hunter stared at him for a few more moments (and was it Levon's imagination, or had Hunter been staring at him a *lot* the last few meetings?), then turned the group's focus back to Jenny.

Levon had to hand it to Hunter; the man knew what he was doing. He never allowed the group to wander off on tangents – sports, politics, the price of movies, whatever – for too long. Every once in a while, sure, because he seemed to sense that, as a whole, they needed a few minutes to release some steam before diving head-first back into the Pit, but the man seemed possessed of his mission: to get all of them to confront the twisted and terrible thing that was haunting their fragile interior worlds.

". . . don't really know what I should say to him," whispered Jenny.

"Do you like him?" asked another member of the group.

"Oh, yes. I mean, well, we've worked together for three or four years now in the property pricing department. I feel like I know him well enough to see him socially, y'know, like in a group for lunch or something, but . . ."

A prolonged silence as Jenny gathered – or tried to avoid – her thoughts, then Hunter chimed in: "But what?"

"I guess that Nick's still too much a part of my everyday life."

"If the guy's any kind of friend at all," said Hunter, "he'll understand." He then addressed the group. "Look, m'droogies, the idea here is not to expunge or even fully overcome your grief – and don't let the pop psychologists blow that kind of smoke up your ying-yangs; you will *never* fully get over your loss – what we're trying to do is simply give *you* the upper hand. That sadness, that feeling of loss, will always be part of you. The goal is for you to learn to control it instead of vice-versa. Okay, wake up your neighbor, I'm done pontificating for now."

The group laughed, and the level of tension in the room dropped considerably. That was another thing about Hunter that Levon had to admire whether he wanted to or not: the man took his mission seriously, but never himself. He always seemed to know just when to let fly with a healthy dose of self-deprecating humor. As a result, the group would probably follow Hunter off the top of the Empire State Building if the man told them it'd be all right. That kind of power was both awe-inspiring and scary as hell.

The soft laughter died down, then Hunter reached over and gave Jenny's hand a squeeze. "Did you talk it over with Tiresias?"

Levon bit down on his lower lip: *Oh, no-no-no-no-no – not the fucking* mouse *again!*

A smile shopping for a new home tried on Jenny's face, decided it felt out of place in that particular neighborhood, and moved on. "I sort of – well, okay, yes, I did talk to him for a few minutes but then I . . . I started to feel kind of . . . of . . ."

"Cliff-Robertson-in-*Charlie*-like?" said Hunter.

Jenny shrugged. "Yeah. But you were right about one

thing though—I didn't feel quite so alone with Tiresias in the house."

"Good." Hunter reached down, gripped the handle, and lifted the typewriter-sized metal cage, setting it gingerly on a nearby empty chair. In the cage, half-buried in the wood-chips and with his butt brushing against the base of the exercise wheel, a chubby brown mouse poked up its head and looked around at the group as if wondering which lucky so-and-so was going to take him home tonight.

Tiresias, sometimes called "Tie" by those group members who'd grown to love him.

"Tie looks like you fed him well," said Hunter.

Jenny blushed a little. "I gave him some extra cheese the other night. But I told him he had to do at least twenty minutes on the wheel."

"I don't think he listened," replied Hunter.

Once more the group laughed; once more Levon pictured them doing a lemming off the top of the Empire State Building; but this time he forgot himself and accidentally joined in the fun. Luckily, no one noticed.

Hunter glanced at his watch, said something about their two hours nearly being up for this week, and asked if anyone had something to add or ask before they broke up.

It happened in the moment between Hunter's looking at his watch and raising his head; for one terrible second in which he feared he'd be forever frozen, the pain in the back of his head came snarling forward, turning every muscle in his body to concrete and gluing his eyelids open, and Levon saw the therapist *alter*: Suddenly Hunter's eyes bulged forward and outward like an insect's, far too large for his head, too large for any *human* head, and Levon thought he was back in the dream, those unhuman almond eyes following his every move, their deep blackness filled not only with coldness but something more underneath, something he dared not try to identify because it would mean staring into them and he knew if he did that he'd be swallowed in their gaze and spend the rest of time as a prisoner screaming behind them, trapped, pounding his fists against the inner-tissue, a child sent away to summer camp pressing his face against the rear window of the school bus as the thing took off while Mommy and Daddy grew smaller and smaller as he was spirited away into the horrifying Unknown where no friends waited.

The moment passed quickly enough, though much of the pain remained, but a thought, unbidden and new, trailed behind it: *I don't belong here; she's not really dead, you know.*

He looked away from the group, focusing his gaze on one of the empty, off-white walls in the church's basement. For some reason, staring at a smooth, softly-colored surface made coming down from a corkscrew easier.

At first he thought that maybe one of the parish childrens' groups had been working on an art project down here, because there was something on the wall that at first looked like a body under a sheet, but on closer examination seemed more like a *bas-relief* sculpture.

Right up until the moment it pulled one hand free and began crawling out from the wall.

– not again, not again, go away, go away, not really there, just a reaction to the headache, like always, so go away, go away, go away –

It paused, long arms and misshapen torso now fully freed from the wall, and turned its oversized head toward him.

Whenever this happened, Levon was always taken by

how much the things seemed more composed of tears or blots of light that floated across his retinas, yet there was a definite *shape* trying to reach corporeal fruition; it had no ears, none of them ever did, and there were flanges of what he assumed was flesh opening in the center of its large oval face . . . and, of course, two areas atop the face where he knew *those eyes* would appear if he stared long enough.

He looked away, took another deep breath, blinked, and looked back to find the wall just as it had been a few seconds before; empty, off-white, hopefully soothing to the eye.

Still, the thought remained: *I don't belong here; she's not really dead, you know.*

It wasn't until he was reaching over the back of his chair for his coat that Levon realized he'd spoken those words aloud.

The group was staring at him again.

Oh, Christ, he thought: *For someone who doesn't want to talk, you're certainly doing enough to attract attention to yourself.*

"Well, well, *well,*" said Hunter. "Did everyone hear that? Garbo talks."

Levon felt his ears growing warm. "I'm, uh . . . I'm sorry. I guess I was just thinking out loud." *I gotta get the hell out of here, get home. Say the magic words: Codeine Pills.*

Hunter persisted. "Then why don't you think out loud and let the rest of us listen? I promise no one in the group will laugh. *Me,* though . . . I take my guffaws where I can get them, but it's nothing personal."

"I, uh . . . I don't really feel like –"

"That's a typical symptom of –"

"– excuse me – lips moving, still talking."

"Which means you're also still breathing, much to your chagrin, I gather."

"Knock it off. Aren't you always telling us that no one should be forced to speak if they don't want to?"

"C'mon," said Cletus Walters, a widower of five years who always sat on Levon's left. "It ain't like any of us've got . . . got a lot to rush home to."

Levon stared into Cletus's tired and worn farmer's face and felt a cloak of sadness drape itself over his shoulders. Why was he behaving this way? These were all good, decent people, and he'd been without any friends for so long . . . maybe he'd just forgotten how to make friends, how to let people in. Or maybe he'd just outgrown seeing the need for any of it.

After several moments of silence and inaction, Hunter said: "Okay, Levon, what now? Do we dare eat a peach, take three giant steps, what?"

Despite his annoyance at being put on the spot like this, Levon couldn't help but stare at the coin that danced gracefully through Hunter's fingers (did the man ever *not* have that thing in his hands?): *red-green-red-green-red-green.*

He was snapped back to the moment by Jenny saying, "We're all here to *listen* to each other, Levon. I mean, this is called a 'support' group. Come on, please?"

Several other members of the group echoed her sentiments.

"Looks like there'll be no clean getaway for you tonight, my friend," said Hunter. "So you might as well 'fess up."

Levon eyed his two aluminum canes with longing.

Had the world ended at that very second, he might very well have cheered.

"Look," he finally managed to get out, "I was just thinking . . . I was just thinking that there's a good chance I'm wasting everyone's time – mine included – by being here." He shrugged. "I don't know, I guess

. . . I guess I've been feeling a bit . . ."

" . . . guilty?" asked Hunter.

Levon started. Hunter had hit a nerve but he was damned if he'd cop to that. "Why would I feel – ?"

"– because you've been attending our sessions every week for five months now, and the only thing you've contributed to any of our discussions is a haze of menthol-flavored cigarette smoke." *Green-red-green-red-green-red.* "You come skulking in here at seven p.m. every Thursday and at exactly nine o'clock you dervish out that door like the Tasmanian Devil hungry for Bugs Bunny's behind, and you have yet to say so much as 'Hi,' 'Bye,' or 'Kiss my middle-aged banonga-loo-loos.' You plant yourself in that same corner and listen to every person in this room attempt to get in touch with their heart so they might, just *might* be able to express the pain that threatens to cripple their every waking moment, but you never join in." *A flash of those huge, insect-black, almond eyes again, then red-green-red-green.* "Are you afraid of being judged, Levon? Of being perceived as weak? We're all weak in some way, so put your ego in park and welcome to the club, pal. If I sound harsh it's only because experience has taught me that the longer a person shields his- or herself with their right to remain silent, the more the Pit consumes of their soul."

"*And* you're a little pissed off," said Cletus.

Hunter shrugged. "Okay – and I'm a little pissed off. Now, Levon – cool name, by the way; I assume your parents were big fans of The Band? – anyway, you can walk out that door and spit in our collective face, or you can say 'hello' and take a chance that we'll listen and care about what's happening inside you."

Defeated – more by guilt than by Hunter's logic – Levon plopped back down into his chair, sighed, and stared silently at the floor for several moments.

"I didn't say you had to spill your guts like this," said Hunter. "You might hurt yourself."

Levon glared at the therapist. "I thought guys like you were supposed to show compassion and understanding. Stop chewing me a new one."

"Tell us what's going on in there and I'll stop being such a prick – though it seems you're doing your best to monopolize that particular franchise."

"Nice rapport you got there, *doc.* How long have you been at this, anyway? Didn't you once say you used to be some sort of mathematician?"

"Yes."

"Why'd you quit?"

"Long division gave me eye-strain and writer's cramp – stop trying the change the subject."

"What do you want to hear, huh? You want me to haul out the sack-cloth and ashes, wring my hands and wail? Beat at my breast? Or do you wanna know how my fucked-up legs are probably never going to get any better than they are right now?"

"I think I can speak for all of us when I say the world weeps over the loss of your ballet career."

"You're being an asshole."

Hunter sighed and looked at his watch. "Will you look at that, Levon? The moment of my death is two minutes closer and you haven't said a thing to justify my using up that time."

"What do you want to know?"

"How about her name?"

"Wh-*what?"*

"Your girlfriend's name, Levon. All we know is that you lost her in the same crash that mangled your legs. You've never told us her name. Why is that? You afraid that actually saying it aloud will open the floodgates?"

Lost her, thought Levon. *He didn't say* she was killed, *he said* lost her. " . . . I don't know," he whispered. Was the *mouse* staring at him, as well?

A note of tenderness crept into Hunter's voice. "I promise on the monthly joke I call a salary that I won't ask anything more of you tonight if you'll just tell us her name."

Levon glared at Hunter, opened his mouth to say what the jerk wanted to hear –

– and felt the air pulled from his lungs in a rush and his mouth go dry and his heart double its beating and something in his gut grow razor-claws that raked across his lower intestine and –

– and it was just a *name,* that was all, two lousy syllables, not all that much, nothing really, so why couldn't he just *say* it and –

– because you haven't even allowed yourself to so much as think *her name since the accident.*

Chalk up another annoying epiphany for Gimp-Boy, the Wonder-Driver.

He shook himself, pulled the stolen air back into his lungs, swallowed what little saliva he could muster, and very slowly, very softly, managed to croak: ". . . Paula."

Hunter stared – *green-red-green-red* – then, eyes not blinking, face not changing expression, nodded and said, "Well, all right, then. Thank you, Levon."

The others offered their thanks and support, as well, and Levon would have been fine if it hadn't been for melancholy old Farmer Cletus – he of the worn face and sad eyes and well-used coveralls that smelled of sweat and the fields and the barn; the man *had* to lean over and put a hand on Levon's shoulder and say, in the kind of voice you imagine a very, very lonely person uses when they've mustered all their courage to beg for some form of human contact: "Sounds like she was a right sweet gal."

And that did it.

Something in Levon tore its chains from the wall

and kicked down a door; try as he did to imprison it again, he started speaking in a rapid, deadly cadence: "She never thought she was beautiful. 'My features are too sharp, they look harsh,' she'd always say. But I never thought so; her features *were* sharp but not in a mean way, y'know? I used to have these dreams, right, where I was trying to sculpt my true love, my soul-mate out of marble, and no matter how hard I tried, I couldn't get to the heart of the mystery that lay hidden in the stone – but I'd keep at it, by God, because I'm a man and no man admits to being defeated by a slab of marble, so there I'd be, chipping away until my entire body'd start to cramp, then a voice behind me would say, 'You keep going like that and there won't be anything left,' so I'd turn around and . . . and there'd be Paula, and *she* was the truth, the *very truth* I was trying to get at in the stone.

"She . . ." He wiped at his nose and almost laughed at this next memory; almost. " . . . she had a slightly oversized nose for such a delicate face – I'm not talking a W.C. Fields honker or anything like that, it was just a fraction too big for her – but the thing is, it fit, it *belonged,* because when you'd meet her, you'd notice that about her nose, about it being a tad too big, but it was as if it were *designed* to draw your gaze to her eyes. God, her eyes. I have never seen such clear, kind, sexy eyes on any person. You know those pictures in storybooks where the sky is this crisp, light, ethereal blue? A perfect, mythic autumn-sky blue, the kind you almost never see in real life? Even *that* paled against the crystal azure of her eyes. I could've swum a hundred raging rivers on the memory of just one glance. And she *listened,* you know? Not just with her ears but with her heart – and not only to what you were saying but to all the unspoken thoughts between the words.

"The best, though, was her hair and voice and the

feel of her skin. Her hair was . . . she wore it parted in the center, okay, cut shoulder-length, and it was this intoxicating combination of black, dark brown, and grey. When the sunlight would fall on it at a certain angle, her hair became silver, black, and gold. Sometimes the sides would flip forward onto her cheeks, and one of the greatest pleasures, one of the profound *privileges* of my life, were those times when I'd reach over and brush back those little hair-flips, then touch her cheek with my hand and just *stay* like that. There are moments now I can still feel the . . . the *ghost* of her skin on my fingertips. Whenever I'd touch her like that, she'd smile and say 'I wish you'd learn to use moisturizer,' in this low, soft, purr-in-the-back-of-her-throat voice. I . . . I miss her so goddamned much that I lay there in bed in the mornings and force myself to think of one, only *one* reason to get up – shit, it doesn't even have to be a *good* reason – and it scares holy hell out of me because it's getting harder and harder to come up with that one reason each morning and pretty soon I'm gonna run out of them and then what's going to happen?"

Tears, unexpected and unwelcome, were coming fast and furious now, drenching his cheeks, damn near blinding him, and through those tears he saw Hunter change again: this time his entire head seemed to shimmer and metamorphose into something large and oval, covered with cold grey flesh that housed even colder black, almond-shaped eyes, and Levon knew that he was seeing for the first time the face of the thing in his dreams, dreams that had begun in the hospital as he spent twenty-two days in a coma, dreams which diminished him even now, sometimes when he was awake, even now, now and forever, amen, and thanks for killing the love of my life, dear Lord. By the way – fuck you, too.

He wasn't even aware that he'd started another cigarette.

"You shouldn't smoke so much," said Jenny tenderly.

And the spell was broken. A breath, a blink, a cough, and Levon's defenses instantly reconstructed their walls.

"I don't have the nerve to shove a twelve-gauge in my mouth so I'm opting to commit suicide on the installment plan. Doesn't leave such a mess on the walls."

Before anyone could respond, he lurched out of his chair, donned his jacket, grabbed his crutches, and made – theoretically, anyway – like the Tasmanian Devil out the door.

He didn't look back when he heard Hunter rush out into the hall, calling, "I don't think this is a good idea, Levon."

He managed to stumble up the stairs and get outside, slamming the church's basement-entrance doors behind him. *Foil* that *clean getaway,* he thought, then did his best to hightail it the half-a-block to the bus stop before he missed the last #19 – which was already pulling up to a line of impatient people. As if conspiring to make the evening an even bigger pain the ass, the sky was dumping down a miserable combination of snow and sleet that transformed the soon-to-be passengers into a cluster of frozen ghosts; it also considerably slowed Levon's efforts to become a ghost himself. His crutches slipped several times and once his balance faltered so badly that he almost went ass-over-teakettle into a line of metal trash cans. Thinking it was better to be safe than splattered, he stopped for a moment, took a deep, cold, freezing-wet breath, and proceeded toward the kiosk ghost-line by sliding instead of lifting his feet.

Winter nights made your mind crazy; he could almost swear that everything in front of him – the passengers, the bus fumes, the snow itself – had simply *stopped.*

"Works for me," he whispered to no one in particular. "At least I'll catch the damned thing."

He might have made it if not for the small patch of black ice that he hit at just the right angle; drum-roll, please: first the crutches went flying sideways, sad aluminum wings too thin for flight, then his feet arced out from under him and before he could yell out for one of the icy ghosts to hold the bus he did a pratfall that would have made Buster Keaton proud.

All he could do was lay there and listen to the bus pull away and stare upward at the winter night sky, unblinking as the sleet and snow covered his body. Maybe he'd freeze to death if he tried hard enough.

Then came the sound of footsteps crunching toward him.

"New hobby?" asked Hunter. "Or is this some radical form of Geek street theater that hasn't caught on in the mainstream yet?"

"If I could reach you, I would hurt you."

"Did you hear that? – the sound of my teeth chattering in fear. Or maybe it's just misdirected flatulence. Want some help rejoining the world of the upright?"

Not waiting for an answer, Hunter reached down and – with one astonishingly strong hand – helped pull Levon to his feet. (The other hand, natch, was busy with the Think Coin: *Green-red-green-red-green* . . .) Levon muttered his thanks, brushed off his coat while Hunter retrieved the prodigal crutches, then stared at the empty space where the bus had been.

"I'm gonna go out on a limb here and guess that you need a lift home?" said Hunter.

"Yes." Short, clipped, angry, that.

"Think you could stand being in a car with me?"

"I suppose."

"I'm touched by your enthusiasm – oh, by the way, you forgot something." He held out Tiresias's cage.

Levon blinked. "You're kidding, right?"

"You know the rules, Levon: the last person in the group to speak before we break up takes Tie home for the week. I assumed that since you made such a dramatic exit you must really want his company."

"I am not taking a goddamned rodent home with me."

Hunter waved a finger at him. "Watch it, you'll hurt his feelings." He pushed the cage closer.

Levon shook his head and gestured with the crutches. "What? You expect me to hold the handle in my teeth?"

"Do that and walk a tightrope at the same time and I think we've found you a new career."

Levon shouldered past Hunter. "Is everything a joke with you?"

"Not always," replied the therapist, falling in step. "With some people, though, it's a defense mechanism."

"How so?"

"If I'm making jokes I'm not rubbing ground glass in their eyes."

Levon stopped. "That a threat?"

"Just trying to get a rise out of you."

Levon grinned (which he didn't want to do), then laughed (which he *really* didn't want to do). "Don't do that to me, doc. I'm not all that sure I *want* to feel better right now."

Hunter considered those words. "I understand. You surprised all of us down there, you know that, right?"

"Guess I've been keeping a bit too much to myself."

Without his even being aware that Hunter had been guiding him, Levon found himself standing by the passenger side of the therapist's car; one moment he'd been over by the church, a good quarter-block away, and then – *blink!* – here in the parking lot.

God, please – not blackouts again. I'll deal with the fucking headaches, okay? Just, please, no more blackouts!

Using his remote, Hunter turned off the car-alarm and unlocked the doors.

Levon just stood there, staring at the handle.

"This is the point where most people get inside," said Hunter.

"Uh-huh."

Snow and sleet accumulated on Levon's shoulders but he made no move to open the door.

Hunter eyes suddenly widened. "Oh, boy – I'm sorry."

"About what?"

"I didn't think. You probably haven't even been *near* a car, let alone inside one, since the accident, have you?"

"Give that man a box of Cubans."

"That's why you take the bus."

Levon shrugged. "I figure the only thing that's going to crumple a city bus is another city bus, a Sherman tank, or a crashing plane."

"Look, Levon, I'm a good driver. I'll go slowly and take side-streets and –"

"Don't coddle me." He yanked open the door and climbed inside. Now if only he could remember to *exhale. . . .*

Levon was a bit shaken by the amount of small yellow Post-Its that decorated the dashboard in an almost perfectly straight line; mathematical equations like (íi3xi3,b=5ñs) and others that were even more indecipherable.

Hunter opened the driver's-side door and saw Levon staring at the equations. "Old habits die hard. That's an older variation on Pythagoras's Triangular Relation theory. Don't you find that exciting? Makes me tingle." He set Tiresias's cage in the center of the front seat. "I forgot my briefcase. Be back in a zero-time blink."

"Huh?"

"Zero-time blink. That's one of them thar snooty mathematician terms." He closed the door, leaving Levon alone with the cold and the snow and –

– and when Levon looked out the driver's-side window he felt his heart wrench loose from its valves and arterial tissues because it was trying to squirt through his ribs.

The world he saw through Hunter's window was not the same one he saw through the car's windshield; the world in front of him was one of night and wind and heavy, wet, hard-driving snow and sleet that clung to every surface it touched, but when he turned his head to the left and looked out Hunter's window, he saw only blackness and stars and the deep country of empty space, as if he were looking through the observation portal of a space shuttle. The view from here told him that he was light-centuries from Earth so don't bother trying to deny it; he couldn't even find any of the familiar constellations which from the beginning of history had been friends and compasses to humankind. He sensed for a terrifying moment that the stars which blazed around him had never before be seen by the unaided human eye. Most of them were concentrated in a glowing belt, broken here and there by ebony bands of obscuring cosmic dust. He wondered if he weren't being given a glimpse of the center of someone's interior galaxy – perhaps even his own – whose true form lie only in the prehistoric depths of the unconscious, but that was bullshit because everything within and without told him that he was *physically* disconnected, so inconceivably removed from the

Solar System that it mattered not a tinker's damn if he were exploring his own interior cosmos or one that had never been glimpsed by even the most powerful of radio telescopes –

– and *had* Hunter become something more in that moment the door closed, a being of grey flesh and black almond eyes and stick-thin, lithe arms and legs? –

– and *were* those more members of the Bas-Relief Gang emerging from the walls of the buildings, the sheets of snow, even the ground surrounding the car, reaching up or out, pulling themselves from the maws like a child forcing the moments of its birth? –

– a breath, a blink, two fingers squeezing the bridge of his nose, and when Levon looked back he saw that the enigmatic galaxy had vanished from Hunter's window, replaced with the same world seen through the windshield.

Leaving him once again alone in the comfortable grip of consensual reality; just himself and the snow and one brown mouse, sitting in a cage.

Those, and his memories . . .

It was not a night for the sadistic absurdity of Death's unwelcome handiwork.

At Paula's request, Levon had attended a performance of Shakespeare's *As You Like It* in Schiller Park. They had been dating for just over three months and this was to be the first time he'd ever seen her on stage. She had spoken often enough about her love of the theater, recounting various experiences – some humorous, others rather terrifying – that she'd had both on the stage and behind the scenes, but she'd not invited him to see her act until tonight.

As he sat down on the sloping green hillside that faced the stage, he couldn't have been any more nervous if he were in the production himself.

The production was pleasant enough, if a tad on the long side. The director had decided to set the show during Colonial times. Paula, according to the cast list in the program, was playing the role of Betsy Ross. Which actual Shakespearean character Betsy Ross was replacing Levon couldn't tell, not being familiar with the Bard's works.

At some point near the end of the first act, one of the leads made a reference to " . . . our dearest Betsy," then pointed toward a stoop-shouldered old woman sitting on a tree stump at the far left side of the stage.

It wasn't just because of the makeup, the spirit gum and gray wig and whatever else she had used to give herself the appearance of age; this was no would-be starlet employing every possible artificial trapping, conveying the essence of old-womanhood through crafty affectation; Paula *was* old. Through some kind of sorcery he hadn't the capacity to comprehend, she had aged fifty years since disappearing to the backstage area two hours ago. No one was *this* good. She was an old woman, one who had nearly been broken by the storms but had managed to persevere, despite all the chaos around her. You could see it in the way she lifted her head, slowly, with hard-earned dignity; an old woman who didn't snap to attention for anyone but made them stand waiting while she decided whether or not they were worth her time; you could tell it in the way she sat with her legs pressed together at the knees, defiant, regal and strong; you knew it by the subtle, nearly imperceptible way her hands trembled when she put down her sewing and let go of the needle – a slight twitch of her index finger, a slow flexing of her thumb, a smooth, liquid unfurling of the muscles beneath her liver-spotted, tissue-paper thin flesh as she lay her hands palms-down on the surface of the flag on which she had been working; all of these nuances and countless others were there, and not in any 1-2-3 manner, not some vain actress moving through a directed series of over-rehearsed, catalogued movements; here was *an old woman,* not ancient by any means, but old nonetheless – and if he'd doubted that she was the real thing, if he'd had any lingering suspicions that all of it was just part of an intricate (albeit damned effective) illusion, if he'd thought that she'd do something – anything – to break the spell – a small, tell-tale gesture that said, *See, I'm still your Paula* – all of it went right down the tubes the second she opened her mouth and spoke her one line because that voice, that weathered, tattered-silk voice that still held the ghost of its bygone youth, that voice of one who'd walked headfirst into life and emerged at the far end a bit worse for the wear but still very much her own person, a voice filled with both wisdom and naïveté with just a raspy touch of playfulness around the edges, this voice told him in no uncertain terms that the Paula he knew and loved was not here at all: She had been replaced for this moment in time – completely, totally, incontrovertibly replaced – by an old woman who'd been summoned forth from her grave somewhere in American history.

He was so proud of her he might have burst wide open right there and then had it not been for the audience applauding at the end of the act.

Afterward he found her backstage, packing her makeup into a plastic tackle box. He came up behind her, put a hand on each of her shoulders, spun her around, and kissed her.

"What was *that* for?" she asked, looking around to make sure no one was staring at them.

"That was one of the most phenomenal things I've ever seen! Do you have any idea how incredible you were? My God, if I hadn't known better, I'd've sworn it wasn't you up there. *Everything* you did was right on the money, was . . . was –"

She laughed and playfully smacked his arm. "Take a tranquilizer already! Sheesh. One lousy line."

"But you –"

"– did it well? Thanks. I'm glad you enjoyed the show and – oh, no you don't. If you want to kiss me again, we have to go somewhere a little more private."

"That's almost coy, coming from you."

"It is? Remind me never to do it again. I'll have to wash my mouth out with vinegar as it is. *Coy*? Never have I shuddered with more horror."

That's when he knew he was going to ask her to marry him, but decided to wait until they were back at her place. Privacy was very important to her. She thought public displays of affection were inappropriate – her one nod to Puritanism – and had told him often enough that things of an intimate nature should be reserved for intimate places; the least he could do, after having practically attacked her backstage, was wait until they were completely alone before asking the most important question a person can ask and another can answer.

While driving to her side of town he once again complimented her performance, this time less effusively and with not as much drooling.

"Thanks," she said. "I've always liked acting. It gives me a chance to change my face, make it prettier or older, threatening or younger. I long ago gave up any hopes of being cast as the ingénue. I don't 'look' right – at least that's what every director I've ever worked with has told me. You can do everything with makeup to a plain face except make it beautiful, and beautiful's the only thing that counts with a 'stage picture.' Which is a nice way of saying that no one will ever cast me as Juliet, damn it. So I have to be content playing mothers, or grandmothers, or colorful eccentrics, or characters who've got no business being in a Shakespearean piece. *Betsy Ross,* for chrissakes!"

"Do you at least get a lot of good supporting roles?"

"Don't I wish. Oh, sometimes, sure, I get a nice meaty role, but mostly what I get is what you saw tonight – one-line throwaway parts. What most theater people call 'stage dressing.'"

"Is it enough?"

She looked down at the makeup case on her lap and shrugged. "Doesn't matter." A sad silence, then: "You know why I do this? Because I like pretending that I'm different people. Someone other than who and what I am. I get to be all the people I wish I were. Might be. Should have been."

"I think who you are is perfect."

"That's sweet, and is probably going to get you laid in about twenty minutes, but it won't help all that much the next time I spend three hours at an audition to end up with one line. Look, most of the time I'm perfectly happy with the way I am but, still, sometimes. . . .

"So I pretend. And I like to think that I actually bring these people to life for a little while, that I lower, I don't know, certain *walls,* and give them safe passage into this world. I used to have this fantasy when I first started out – *still* have it, sometimes – that these characters I played actually hung around after the show closed, that they really existed, only on a different plane, you know? Like ghosts. And all of them look a little like me. Isn't that a scary thought? Dozens and dozens of ghosts roaming the night out there, touring all their various worlds, and all of them looking a little like me."

He laughed as he reached over to touch her cheek. "How do I know you're not one of them?"

Silence. A thin, wistful smile.

Then: "You don't."

And that's when the blinding bright lights exploded through the front of the car and glass blew against his face and the metal of the car came momentarily to life just long enough to release its death-screams and –

"–The next thing I knew there was this chainsaw-sound and when I managed to get one of my eyes open, I saw the guys from the fire department. They were cutting me out of the car – what was *left* of it, anyway."

Dear God, when had Hunter come back? Levon couldn't remember the car starting or leaving the parking lot or even pulling onto the road. How long had they been moving?

That's twice in one night, Einstein. How much longer you planning to wait before telling someone about it – until you find yourself up in some tower with a high-powered rifle, trying to make the Bad Things leave you alone?

"The truck crossed the center line and hit you head-on?" asked Hunter.

Levon started, then quickly composed himself. "Yeah. Later, one of the police officers told me that the poor guy had been on the road for over thirty hours. I guess he fell asleep at the wheel. When he hit us, he shoved us along for a good two, three hundred yards. The only thing that stopped us was the side of the hill."

Hunter visibly winced. "Jesus. You were really pinned in, then."

"I should've been killed," whispered Levon, shaking his head in disgust. "Sometimes I wish I had been killed. Even with the goddamn air-bags and reinforced side-doors and all that state-of-the-art what-have-you . . . the truck crushed the car like it was an aluminum can. It took them three hours to cut me out of the wreckage."

He watched Hunter carefully. The man took in all the information, then nodded once, bit his lower lip, and said, "And Paula?"

"She was gone."

"I'm so very, very sorry."

Levon shook his head and wiped at his eyes, noting as he did so that Hunter had given his Think Coin to Tiresias and the mouse was playing with it. A shared nervous compulsion between man and rodent. Ought to have been inspiring; Levon found it nearly surreal.

"Back at the meeting," continued Hunter, "you said something about how you shouldn't really be there, about how Paula –"

"– wasn't really dead?"

"Yes."

Levon leaned over – not too far, just enough so that Hunter would know he was serious about this next thing: "What I tell you now, it stays between us. I don't want you blindsiding me with it at one of the meetings some night."

No jokes or smiles or smirks this time; Hunter gave Levon a very serious, very intense glance, and nodded his head once, quickly and firmly.

Levon sat back and looked at Tiresias; the mouse had taken the Think Coin over to the exercise wheel and somehow managed to wedge it between two of the spokes so that, as he ran inside the wheel, the coin spun 'round and 'round.

"That's a fairly clever mouse."

"Tiresias is full of surprises," said Hunter proudly. "He notices and understands more than you'd think

. . . but that's not what you wanted to tell me, was it?"

Levon chewed on one of his thumbnails and stared out the windshield; the way the snow was blowing toward them it looked as if they were on the verge of breaking the speed of light; all the stars were trying desperately to catch up with them.

"When the fire department and paramedics and all the other crews were finally able to cut me out and dislodge the car, Paula was gone. Not *dead,* you understand – *gone.*" Saying it out loud like that still gave him a mondo case of the willies. "I was conscious for maybe a total of forty minutes after they got me out, then it was off to La-La Land for three weeks . . . but I was around and lucid long enough to hear all of the talking. They were going on like I'd been the only person in the car! I finally managed to get my tongue to work well enough to tell a paramedic that Paula had been in there with me, and the guy gave me one of those patronizing smiles like he just *knew* I was delirious.

"When I came out of the coma, I told as many people as I could about Paula. The doctors and nurses all listened and were sympathetic, but none of them *did* anything. Not one of them told the authorities. Even the cops who came by to take my statement gave me these pitying looks – 'Poor guy got himself too many screws knocked loose in the wreck' – but I finally raised enough hell and stuck to my story long enough that somebody looked into it, because a few days before I was released a couple of detectives and some big-wig expert from the Highway Patrol came by with this thick file of reports.

"There was no physical evidence to suggest that anyone else had been in the car that night. My blood, my bone fragments, hair strands, saliva, shit – but *just mine.* Nothing of Paula had been found in the wreckage. *Nothing.* I know damn well she was in the car with me because the second before the truck slammed into us she grabbed my leg and said something like, 'Not with a whimper,' but . . . but between the time the truck hit us and the car slammed into the side of the hill, Paula . . . she . . ."

" . . . disappeared?" said Hunter.

"Loony-Tunes, right? But, yes. She just" – he snapped his fingers – "vanished."

"You were able to prove that you left the park together that night, right? I mean, the other cast members had to've –"

"Oh, yeah, there were dozens of people who confirmed my story, all the times matched up, cha-cha-cha . . . but there was no Paula in the car. They searched for a while but never found any trace of her."

Hunter shook his head as he mulled over the facts. "A collision like that, there was no way she could've been thrown free and not suffer severe body trauma."

"So what happened to her, huh? Got any textbook theories on where the love of my life went?"

Hunter said nothing, sensing, perhaps, that Levon wasn't expecting an answer and would be really angry if one were offered.

"I knew her exactly ninety-four days," Levon whispered. "But it was enough to know I wanted to spend the rest of my life with her. I think we'd only said 'I love you' to each other three or four times, if that – but *man,* each time it was like breaking open a diamond and hearing it play the music of the spheres. Ninety-four days."

"Hardly any time at all," said Hunter. "God, how that must hurt. I mean, it's one thing to lose someone you've spent decades with – not that *that* isn't its own special corner of hell – but I've always thought it must be worse in some ways to lose someone who you've only started to truly love, on whom you're still high enough to revel in all the mundane day-to-day discoveries and believe in magic again. It's not just the physical and emotional loss, it's being robbed of all the . . . magnificent possibilities that might have lain ahead for the two of you."

For a few minutes after that, they drove in near-total silence. Levon braced himself for the world outside the car to alter again and wondered if he should tell Hunter about that, maybe even the dreams about the eyes, but then decided on something else.

Or maybe that something else made the decision for him.

"You know I cried on our first date?"

"Please tell me it wasn't during or after sex," said Hunter. "That'd be just too damn sad and I'd have to pull over and make you get out of the car. It's a He-Man guy thing."

Levon grinned, silently thanking the therapist for his deft timing. "I suppose it wasn't *technically* our first date – we'd had lunch together several times – but this was our first good-gosh adult nighttime date. I even wore a tie. We went to this festival of short films at the Grandview Theater. You ever been there?"

"Several times."

"Great movie house. Paula liked that they used real butter on their popcorn. Anyway, they showed something like nine short movies, none of them longer than ten minutes, until the last one, *The Red Balloon.*"

"Oh, that is one *great* flick," said Hunter. "My favorite movie, in fact."

"I thought it was sweet in a sad kind of way, until those last few minutes. You know, you watch this lonely little kid wandering the Paris streets with this miraculous red balloon following him like it knew it was the only friend the kid had, then at the end that group of bullies burst the balloon and here's this poor kid, kneeling over the remains of his precious friend and crying –"

Hunter chimed in with tremendous enthusiasm. "– ah, but *then* all of the balloons everywhere in the city escape from their owners and go soaring off to the boy, and they wind their strings around him and lift him up higher and higher, and there he is at the end, flying like a cherub up, up, up into the bluest effing sky you've ever seen –"

"– *God,* yes! Man, how I cried. I couldn't figure out why, I just knew that I was embarrassed as hell. I thought for sure she'd dump me right there on the spot, but she kissed my cheek and took my hand and we snuck out before the lights came up. She drove my car back to my place because I was still pretty wrecked, I felt like an idiot, and then she touched my hand and said, 'You didn't have a lot of fun when you were a kid, did you?' and I said no, I hadn't, I'd been a skinny little geek with thick glasses and crooked teeth and had mom who never bought any clothes for me that *weren't* plaid – you might as well have slapped a sign on my back saying 'Dear Bullies: Please Taunt or Beat the Piss out of Me Any Chance You Get' – but Paula, she listened and held my hand and then gave me the sweetest smile I've ever gotten from another person. 'You should have had your own red balloon,' she said. 'You should have been given a moment like that boy's in the movie, to known that glory, to feel that God is just, to pour the sky into a silver chalice and drink it down. I'm sorry you were so lonely as a kid, but you know what? Even though we haven't known each other all that long, I think I don't want you to ever feel that way again.' We pulled up in front of my house after that but she wouldn't let me get out of the car. She turned on the radio and the station was playing The Beatles' "The Long and Winding Road" and the waterworks came on again – I swear the fuckin' universe was out to get me that night. Couldn't have been some kick-ass Led Zeppelin tune, or The Who or "Born to be Wild" – I'd've settled for K.C. and the Sunshine Band . . . but, no, it *had* to be John and Paul's toe-tapping ode to chronic melancholia. Of all the music I remember from when I was growing up, that song was the one that, in my mind, summed up my childhood and adolescence. Depresses the living shit out of me every time I hear it, yet I *have* to listen to the whole thing. Paula started to change the station and I asked her not to – and when the song was over – you know, that last, unbelievably sad chord – she pulled me close and held me . . . her breath was so warm and gentle it felt like sunlight on my neck . . . then she whispered, 'May I be your red balloon?'

"Corny as hell, I know, but no one had ever said anything so loving and tender to me before – or since, for that matter – and I just . . . crumpled."

Hunter, expressionless, said: "You must be a riot at parties."

"You ought to see what I can do with a lampshade."

They neared Levon's corner, and Hunter slowly made the turn.

"If you were driving any slower I could outrun you on my crutches."

"One more crack like that and you might have to."

The two men looked at one another and smiled.

When they at last pulled up in front of Levon's darkened house, Hunter put the car in park, and turned toward his passenger. The grin on his face told Levon that the therapist knew something he didn't.

"What?"

"Who have you been talking to for the last few minutes?"

Levon started to reply, then realized the reason for

the grin: for the last fifteen minutes, he'd been talking to both Hunter *and* Tiresias.

"Oh, just shoot me now," he groaned.

Hunter burst out laughing. "I told you, didn't I? Tiresias has that effect on people."

"He's still just a mouse."

"Is he?"

Levon's reply was an amused/annoyed stare.

"It seems like you're feeling a little better," said Hunter.

"Oddly enough, yes – but only a little." He looked out the window. "House keeps getting smaller and smaller, no matter how much stuff I get rid of." He turned back to Hunter. "Don't worry – there aren't any exposed ceiling beams that could take my weight. I've looked."

"Come on, then" said Hunter, grabbing the handle of Tiresias's cage. "I'll help you get up the steps and inside."

"Exactly how many times do I have to tell you that I am *not* taking that mouse? Give me a number or take a bribe, just shut up about it already."

Hunter reached into his coat pocket and pulled out a business card. "I'm going to give you an option that I've never offered to any group member before. That card is my private number, rings right into my bedroom. You put that in your pocket and you keep Tiresias for tonight. If having him with you doesn't help, if he doesn't ease your loneliness so much as a fraction, then you call me in the morning and I'll come get him. Fair enough?"

Levon considered it, then nodded, taking the card. "I suppose it's the least I can do. You *did* give me a lift, after all."

"Oh, good, guilt – the great motivator. But the snow's getting heavy and I'm tired so I'll take it and settle for lecturing you about it next week." He offered his hand.

Levon shook it.

That's when he knew that some part of his mind must have sneaked away without so much as a Dear-John note, because even though he could see that Hunter's hand was just your normal, everyday-guy's hand, it *felt* as if it were three times bigger than it was, with fingers like long, fleshy twigs.

Time to go.

Hunter released Levon's hand. "Let's get you two inside."

"My first houseguest in over two years, and it's a rodent. Is my life working out, or what?"

"Give him a chance, all right?"

"Okay."

Tiresias, like an actor responding to his cue, padded over to the exercise wheel, dislodged the coin from between the spokes, then shoved it through the bars of the cage and into Hunter's waiting hand.

Flip/twirl: *Red-green-red-green-red-green . . .*

Levon began to wonder if Hunter played with the damn thing in his sleep.

Tiresias probably know the answer to that.

Maybe he'd ask the mouse about it later . . .

It finally took two-and-half codeine tablets to make the headache go away, an by that time Levon was more than a bit loopy – not that he minded all that much. Since the hospital, he'd come to the conclusion that the majority of pain medication doled out by physicians didn't actually do anything to relieve the pain, they just made you feel so wonky that you didn't *mind* the pain so much.

He was sitting on the edge of the couch, staring out the window at the snow- and-ice-covered trees in his backyard, wondering what most of the forest animals did to stay warm when the whether got this cold.

Eventually, he turned toward Tiresias, whose cage he'd set on a nearby end-table.

The mouse was all at attention, sitting up on its back legs, whiskers twitching as it watched him with oddly *aware* eyes, its tiny hands folded and resting neatly on its belly. Levon could swear that its small fingers (were they even *called* fingers?) drummed rhythmically from time to time, as if the mouse were growing impatient: *Okay, this was fun – mark the use of past tense – what do we do next? Please, let's do something else.*

Levon laughed – more at himself than the mouse – and lay back for a moment.

The first things he focused on were the bookshelves and the small music-box Paula had given him, which sat up on the shelf where Paula kept all her Shakespeare volumes.

"Oh, man."

Tiresias at once sat up, ears twitching straight and high, whiskers frozen, hands unmoving: *Is this it? Is this that* something else *I requested earlier?*

"Do not look at me in that tone of voice," Levon muttered to the mouse.

Tiresias's upper lip curled slightly: *Don't talk to me with that look in your eyes.*

"Understood." He sat up, leaned closer to the window, and reveled in the clearness of the winter-night sky. The sleet and snow had ceased over ninety minutes ago. Now the world of ten-forty p.m. was an ice sculpture through his window, lit by hundreds of glittering, cold stars in an even colder heaven.

He looked over, saw that Tiresias was leaning forward, trying to get his head through the bars – *Gimme a look, c'mon, I wanna see!* – and so hoisted the cage over and rested it on his lap.

He hated to admit it, but both Hunter and Jenny Collins were right; the place *did* feel a little less lonely with the mouse here.

Levon poked the tip of his index finger through the bars; Tiresias immediately took hold of it in his tiny hands, puffed a few breaths on it, then began chewing it affectionately in the same lazy, painless, affectionate way a cat sometimes will.

"Sorry that I've been ignoring you," whispered Levon. "Guess I've just been sitting here staring out at the night, at the stars, ruminating. Do you mind sitting here with for a little while? I find that I'm thinking of all the people I know who aren't here any longer. My dad, Mom, a couple of guys I was close with in college who both died a few years ago, my Uncle Johnny . . . and Paula. A trainload of some of the most terrific people you'd ever have known . . . if you'd have ever met them. I wish I could make you understand how wonderful all of them were, how much I love them, how much I miss them – and, *God,* I do. So here we sit."

He lifted the cage until it was level with his face. "So do me a favor, will you, Tiresias? If your heart can understand, and if it's big enough to spare a moment, give a nod and a smile for all the good ones who spent a part of their lives making mine richer and fuller because of their having been in it. Will you do that for me? Because they're all gone now, and the only way I can think of to tell them how much I miss them is to sit here nights and send them a moment of kind thought and hope . . . hope it'll find its way over to the other side of the stars where they're waiting . . . where *I hope* they're waiting. . . ."

He fell silent after that, unaware that he'd lowered

the cage back onto his lap until he felt Tiresias patting his finger with his tiny mouse hands in an unnerving *there-there-it's-all-right* way.

"Little man, what do you know?"

Tiresias looked up at him and seemed to shrug.

"Hey, I know, how's about we play *True Confessions* for a bit?" He carried Tiresias's cage over to the bookshelf and lifted it high enough so that the mouse had a good look at the music box: one raggedy-ass looking clown, smiling as if someone had just stuck a gun in his back and told him to act natural, standing on the dais and holding the string of a red balloon that hovered over his head.

"You know this goddamn thing hasn't worked since I got back from the hospital? No, really. It used to start up if I so much as *breathed* too hard, but now . . . and, yes, it's wound up and no, the little 'pause' switch on the back isn't set in place, so what you're looking at is a music box that ought to be playing right now but isn't." Levon stomped his foot a couple of times, then picked up the music box and shook, then set it down just a little too hard.

"See? Nothing. And the weird thing is, Paula and I used to set this thing off all the time, even when I was certain I hadn't wound it. At first –" He laughed a somewhat dirty laugh. "– at first, we'd be making love on the couch and all of a sudden the thing'd start playing – man, that was enough to scare the stiffy off a dead man. After a while, though, it seemed like it'd start playing whenever the two of us were in this room together. I kind of figured that it was the Universe's way of telling us that we belonged together, you know? That as long as we stayed by each other's side, nothing bad would ever really happen.

"Paula got that for as a birthday present. I had no idea what to say to her when I saw it. Ugliest piece of crap I ever laid eyes on, but it was the only one she found that played 'The Long and Winding Road.' She figured that if I heard that song coming out of something this ridiculous and pathetic, that maybe it'd lose its hold on me. God bless pop-psychology, eh?"

He found himself staring at the Shakespeare volumes.

"No one ever cast her as Juliet, Tie. Damn it. And we once –"

The words died in his throat. It seemed far too intimate a thing to bring forward.

He'd decided to try something unabashedly romantic on her last birthday, so he'd sent flowers to her at work and waited until he was sure she'd received them, then called her and, without saying so much as 'Hello,' said: "'Give me my Juliet; and when she shall/die/Take her and cut her out in little stars/And she will make the face of heaven so fine/That all the world will be in love with the night.'"

For a moment she was silent on the other end of the line, and Levon's heart jammed up into his throat because he thought for a moment that he'd actually moved her, but then she made a sound, softly, as if she were trying to hold it back.

She was laughing.

"Oh, baby," she said, "I'm sorry. This is so sweet of you, really, but . . ."

"But my ego hasn't been shattered into enough pieces? Pardon me now whilst I go swallow some lye."

"Don't pout. You're sexy when you pout and I'm not there to take advantage of it."

"Then what's so funny?"

"The quote isn't Romeo's. It comes from part of a speech Juliet gives to her nurse in Act Three."

"I was positive that I read it right, that it was Romeo."

"Nope, sorry – Juliet. I'll show you later . . . when I thank you for the flowers and the great, earth-shaking sex."

"What earth-shaking sex?"

"That would be telling . . ."

Standing in his living room now, staring at the volumes, he whispered, "She was right, it wasn't Romeo." He looked down and saw Tiresias staring up at him with a *What-the-hell-are-you-going-on-about?* look on his face.

"Nothing," he said. "Nothing at all."

In sleep he surrendered to the chill timelessness that always accompanies grief. The place in his heart where once existed the love for Paula was silently, stealthily replaced by a lonely aching that filled every crevice of his body.

He awakened to look down upon his sleeping self. He saw a man isolated, apart; ineffective and meaningless, being watched over by the silent sentinel of one brown mouse, sitting in a cage.

Do you wish you were a man? he wondered, but Tiresias offered no reply.

A blink, a sigh, a shiver, and Levon was lying in the bed once again, reunited with his flesh.

He stared at the ceiling, feeling overwhelmed and invaded, as if another Self, a sad, broken thing that had lain dormant for so long, impatient and inaccessible, was insinuating itself into his psyche. Pale moonlight like a beam from a projector shone through the window, alighting on the full-length mirror hanging on the closet door.

In this bed, he was alone.

But not so in the mirror's reflection.

Paula, her crystal azure eyes radiant, was lying next to him there.

He wondered if he should chance touching her –

the Self in the mirror did the same things he did, their movements and gestures synchronized like two Olympic swimmers; if he were to make that Self caress her, would he himself feel the warmth of her lips, the smoothness of her skin, the ordered, necessary, unavoidable erotic truth that was her body? He'd always felt that way. Every time he saw her, every time they kissed, every time he caught a scent of her perfume that entered a room just before she did, he was amazed at the rush of emotions within him. Being with her wasn't like having a fantasy come true before he was ready for it; it was like having a fantasy come true before he'd even had the fantasy.

I swear it was Romeo who said it.

Whatever makes your world right, Levon. Now shut up and snuggle and go to sleep.

In the mirror, he put his arm around her, and they slept as one.

He heard the first plaintive morning song of a bird filter in. Stumbling like a drunkard, he lurched out of bed and to the window, rolling up the blind.

Outside it was 5 a.m. purple-gray; dawn just creeping in, night not quite finished with the world yet. A thin layer of mist enshrouded the yard as a dispirited breeze sloughed its way through the trees. Dewdrops glistened on every surface, shimmering at the tips of leaves.

She had always loved this time of night, this time of morning.

He closed his eyes and pressed his head against the damp window glass. The contrast of its icy temperature against his own feverish one jarred him and he pulled away, snapping open his eyes.

She stood behind him in the window's reflection,

turned inverted in the mirror's reflection, one reflecting the other, an endless line of ghost-Paula's alternating perspective; naked, her hair tumbling down over her shoulders, a dark velvet cradle. He watched as her arms slipped around him, her fingers twirling patterns into his sparse, matted chest hair, then gliding down, down, her fingertips brushing over his nipples as they swept down, slowly down, teasingly down, pausing playfully as she lay her cheek against his bare shoulder, then rolling her head around so her lips kissed the nape of his neck, then one of her hands reached below his waist with craving and purpose; he arched his back to make it easier for her, not daring to turn around because he knew she'd be gone, only in this amorphous reflection could they be together, so he was content to watch as she kissed his neck and rubbed his stomach and massaged his morning erection in a way that always drove him into a frenzy –

– there. Between a couple of ice-sheened trees. A lithe grey figure.

Then another, near the small sloping hill that led down to a frozen stream.

Then many of them, it seemed, or perhaps just one doing its imitation of an electron, jumping from point to point without crossing the space between.

Suddenly terrified, he reached out for Tiresias's cage and accidentally knocked over a plastic container of foot powder, spilling it everywhere.

"Shit," he muttered. Paula's ghost was now gone and he felt alone, but before he could turn away from the window and start cleaning up his mess, one of the figures stepped from the trees and walked into the center of his backyard.

Tall, it was, and mottled-grey of skin, with long, quadruple-jointed fingers and legs thin as vines . . .

. . . and bulging, black, almond-shaped insect eyes.

One of the Bas-Relief Gang, formed from the ice and snow.

Levon closed his eyes and once again pressed his head against the coldness of the window glass, but this time when he opened his eyes the illusion hadn't altered, not one little bit. The creature still stood down below in the yard, and its unnatural shape and height and features should have been enough to send him screaming into the next room, to force him to grab the phone and call Hunter and say, "Okay, time to send me to the bin, doc!"

Should have been, but it wasn't.

Staring into the same eyes he'd been seeing in his dreams, Levon realized that what he'd at first mistaken for coldness was a loneliness and longing that defied categorization; here was a thing in near-unspeakable emotional pain, fighting with everything it had to keep that particular beast chained down so that it could at least find one reason – not even a *good* one – for going on.

But even what he saw in the creature's eyes did not move or frighten him more than what it was holding in one of its hands.

A string attached to a red balloon hovering over its head.

He turned away from the window and everything happened very quickly after that:

He saw that Tiresias's cage door was open and the mouse was gone;

He saw a small trail of mouse-shaped, powdery footprints leading across the floor into the hall;

He heard the front door being unlocked and someone – or *something* – enter the house;

He heard the music box start playing;

And then a loud *whump!* As something heavy hit the downstairs floor.

He looked around in panic for something that he could use as a weapon – it seemed to him there should have been a stick, a cane, *something* – found nothing that could even be remotely dangerous, and so settled for yanking the small bedside lamp from its table, hoping that he could get decent aim at the skull of the intruder.

He took the steps three at a time, then jumped the last four, landing halfway into the living room in a near-perfect bent-knee squat and thinking: *What's wrong with this picture?*

The front door stood open just a crack, as if the intruder had hastily tried to close it –

– *but on its way in or out?* thought Levon, moving forward.

He placed his hand against the door and pushed it closed, noting – but not believing – the small pair of tiny hand-prints he saw on the brass knob.

Right, Tiresias just jumped *up here and opened the door.*

The sound of rustling paper, and Levon whirled around, snapped on the overhead lights, and saw –

– nothing.

The living room appeared to be empty.

So what had made that noise?

Walking very slowly, he crept around the tables and chairs, then the couch, and just as the music box stopped playing he saw Tiresias at the base of the bookshelf, sitting on a page of an opened Shakespeare volume – one of several that littered the floor.

The mouse stared at him, twitched its whiskers, then slapped one hand onto the page.

Levon stared at it.

Tiresias pulled back, made a soft huffing sound, then slapped both its hands onto the page, as if saying: *Really ought to take a look at this, pal.*

Levon knelt down and gently lifted Tiresias onto his

shoulder. The mouse positioned itself so that it too could have a good view of what Levon was about to see.

Lifting the volume so as not to lose the place, Levon at once saw the powdery prints that Tiresias had left by a certain passage of monologue:

Give me my Juliet; and when she shall die,
Take her and cut her out in little stars
And she will make the face of heaven so fine
That all the world will be in love with the night . . .

"This is wrong," he whispered to Tiresias. "I mean, this is what I *thought* it was, but she showed me this passage in at least seven different volumes, and it's Juliet who says this about Romeo – 'when *he* shall die' – to her nurse. This is . . . this Act Four, and that's wrong." He slammed closed the book and saw the hand-print that seemed seared into the cover.

A large hand, with quadruple-jointed fingers.

He dropped the book as if it were covered in fresh vomit.

"Okay, time to go, that's it, where's – ? Oh, yeah, I keep the phone *over there.* Come on, Tie, let's go call the Twinkie Mobile to come take me to the Happy Place."

He grabbed up the phone and punched in Hunter's number.

It wasn't just the prints and the book and the figure in the back yard; there was something else wrong here, something he couldn't quite get a fix on – and it seemed to him he *ought* to know what it was that was . . . missing. Yeah, that was it – something had been subtracted from the known whole of his world.

"Hello?" said the therapist in a groggy, tired voice.

"Hi, Doc, it's me."

"Levon. Still say that's a damned cool name."

"Could you maybe say it over here or at the hospital or something? I'm having a major freak-out here and if it doesn't stop soon I really, really, *really* think I'm going to be in some big trouble."

"Hold on, Levon. I'll be there right away," said Hunter.

"'Right away'? Could you be a little more specific? I don't deal well with the willies."

"I'll be there sooner than you'd think."

"How soon do you think that might be?"

A pause; then: "Turn around."

Levon did, and damn near rammed faces with Hunter, the man was standing so close.

"You should see your face," said Hunter, still flip/twirling his Think Coin. "Bo-Bo the Dog-Faced Boy appeared more intelligent. Got any beer? I prefer imported to domestic but I won't pick nits."

"How the fuck did you do that?"

"Learn enough about *true* Time/Space Relativity and you'll come to realize that physical distance is just an illusion, unlike my thirst. Why am I still not holding a beer?"

"In the 'fridge. Help yourself."

"I will – and by the way, you're taking this surprisingly well. I thought you'd be huddled screaming in the corner."

"Thank you."

"All part of the treatment."

Hunter retrieved his beer and came back into the living room. "I assume you saw your visitor in the back yard?"

Levon could barely nod his head.

"I'll take that to mean 'yes.' Okay, my friend, sit yourself down and listen; there's not a lot of time."

Levon did not so much sit as collapse onto the

couch. Tiresias remained firmly attached to his shoulder, all the time patting away at the side of his neck: *It's okay, it's okay, don't worry.*

Hunter picked up the television remote and turned on the set. "Remarkable apparatus, a television, don't you think?"

Levon shrugged, found his voice. "I don't watch it so much these days."

"Pity. You've got a nice, clear picture there, to boot. Great beer, by the by."

"You gonna talk about cable and brew or is there something else on your mind?"

Hunter grinned. "Look at the television, Levon – yeah, I know, a re-run of *The Brady Bunch,* but that's not the point. The point is that every time you turn on the TV, an electron gun in the back set fires out hundreds of billions of electrons that hit that screen and give you a clear picture of Jan doing her 'Marsha-Marsha-Marsha!' bit. But the thing is, there is nothing programmed into any single electron which tells it that it has to hit a certain section of the screen. You following me so far? I could start again and talk slower."

"I think I'm with you."

"Good. That'll make the rest of this easier." Hunter shimmered in the glow of the set, becoming a thing like that which waited in the back yard, then Hunter again, then the creature, Hunter, on and on. "Now, since the electrons have no way of knowing what part of the picture they're supposed to reproduce on that screen, how do you suppose you even *get* a picture?"

"Blind shit-house luck?"

"Close. You get a picture because you *expect* to get one. You are what physicists call 'the Observer,' and by turning on the TV and *deciding* that you're going to a picture, you collapse the wave function."

"What's that?"

"The wave function? Hmm . . . How to sum it up briefly – but hark, the next beer calls me." Hunter drained the can he was holding, then got himself another one. How he managed to open it with his other hand busy flip/twirling the coin, Levon couldn't imagine – unless the guy used his teeth.

"What I just did? That's a good example of collapsing a wave function. You see, we collapse wave functions every second of every day – do we sit, stand, cross the street, eat a peach, make that call? The wave function – despite what a lot of scientists say – does not represent *probability* but *possibility*. Here I sit; do I drink this beer or not? Do I set it down or throw it across the room, ruining that Oriental rug hanging on your wall? – I assume Paula picked that out – anyway . . . what to do with the beer? An endless choice of possibilities, of roads not yet taken. So what do I do? Let's say I drink." He took a sip of the beer. "And, thus, I collapse the wave function; a choice has been made, there are no other possibilities that can be chosen for that moment, for that moment has now passed and a whole different set of wave functions awaits us in this new moment. Since the quantum wave function represents the possibility of observing an event, the collapse means that the possibility has changed from less than certain to *certainty*. Still with me?"

"Fuck, I don't know."

"Eloquence is your middle name."

Levon rubbed his eyes. "Would you *please* stop twirling that damn coin through your fingers? It's getting on my nerves."

Another grin. "Well, I'll stop with the finger stuff, but . . ." Hunter flexed his fingers and lay his hand on his lap.

The coin, however, remained in the air next to him, twirling in circles as if it were still in his hand.

Levon stared at it for a moment, then reached out to snatch it from the air.

The coin moved out of his reach.

He rose from the couch, tried again to grab the thing, and again it moved out of his reach.

"This could get seriously comical if you don't stop trying to grab hold of that damn thing," said Hunter.

Levon reluctantly sat back down. "Is this some kind of magic trick?"

Hunter seemed offended. "That's right, you nailed me, pal! Nothing up my sleeve, but watch and I'll pull a rabbit out of my ass – *hell, no,* it's not a trick! Give me some credit."

"What's going on?" Levon's voice broke on the last word, and he had to choke down the grief and fear and confusion.

Hunter reached over and gave his shoulder a squeeze while Tiresias continued patting Levon's neck: *There, there; there, there.*

"You'll understand soon enough, I promise." Then Hunter put out his hand and the coin came back to him and the flip/twirling started all over again: *red-green-red-green-red.*

"Let me ask you something, Levon: what do you suppose happened to all the other possibilities once I took a sip of that beer?"

" . . . I dunno . . . they ceased to exit?"

Hunter shook his head. "No. They simply had no place in this universe at that moment."

"So. . . ?"

"So they were freed to be a part of other, countless possible universes, and that's where they went."

"You're talking about . . . about parallel universes?"

Hunter nearly sneered. "Oh, Christ, not you, too!" He began to pace about the room. "I'm sorry, but that term pisses me off. Too many physicists with their heads up their bungholes and *way* too many science fiction books and movies who base their research – providing they actually *do* any – on the conclusions drawn by those bunghole-dwellers. No, not parallel – that implies that they run side-by-side-by-side, that there's some sort of physical distance separating them. No, what they actually be called are *simultaneous* universes.

"Imagine you're in a movie theater, okay, and you're sitting there with your popcorn, Coke, maybe a hot dog – I like hot dogs myself – anyway, there you are, and you're looking at the one big screen. Now imagine that the movie starts, only instead of one film being projected onto the screen, there are hundreds, thousands, *millions* of different films running at the same time . . . only you can't see them. Some apparatus in you can only see one movie at a time, even though all the others are up there, too. *That's* how this universe – and all other possible universes – is constructed. But because you *expect* to see the new Pacino flick, that's what you see. You made that choice, you collapsed that wave function."

"Okay. . . ?" Levon was getting really pretty seriously scared shitless by now. If it hadn't been for Tiresias's reassuring presence, he might have lost it altogether.

Hunter looked like a man possessed as he continued. "All right, friend, now we get to the good stuff. Why this coin in my hand, and why Tiresias? Blame Einstein. He rejected the idea of 'parallel' universes that were created by collapsing wave functions because he didn't believe – and this is his actual example – that a mouse could bring about a radical change in the structure of reality simply by observing it. Wrong! See, old Albert made the conclusion based on his belief that – just like your sitting in a theater that's showing a million movies all at the same time but only seeing one – a mouse doesn't possess the ability to tell the difference between one branch of reality and another, and since, according to Einstein, there's no wave function present in a mouse's perception, there's nothing to collapse." He reached over and took Tiresias in his free hand, then held his coin hand directly across from the mouse, who seemed entranced.

"Say this coin in its present state represents four possible universes: Universe Heads, Universe Green, Universe Tails, Universe Red. Why doesn't Tiresias just pick one and be off on that particular collapsed wave to whatever possible universe awaits beyond the scrim? Because he knows that we *all* exist as conspiracies of simultaneous universes. All possible worlds are all around us, all the time, only we don't realize that. In his own innocent, fuzzy little way, Tiresias does. All the experiences that we say are happening in the here and now are also happening in the other universes, only with slight differences . . . yet the further you journey through the various possible universes, the more radical those differences become, because endless probability waves that *never existed in this time and place* have been collapsed, giving way to new possible universes-within-possible-universes, all of them overlapping simultaneously.

"Tiresias observes this coin which represents four separate universes, yet he doesn't split into four mice. Why? Because for him, the quantum conspiracy is total: He sees a coin, and that's it. For Tiresias, the four universes are superimposed, every movie running at the same time – the four universes are already merged into one."

He sounded like a raving lunatic, yet his words were beginning to make a gonzo sort of sense to Levon. "So what you're saying is . . . is . . ."

"What I'm saying, Levon, is that out there in the

myriad of simultaneous universes, there are beings who are, for lack of a better ready metaphor, the Projectionists. It's their duty to keep all of the possible worlds hidden from one another, because the inhabitants of each one could not deal with that knowledge, with that vision. They chart the splits in the branches of reality, they tally up the collapsed wave functions, they observe the Observers."

"Wh-what are they?"

Hunter shrugged. "Call them aliens, angels, the Old Ones, the First Ones – just don't think of them as little grey intergalactic proctologists who go around snatching up hayseeds from Kansas cornfields at four in the morning – though, unfortunately, some of them still do that; old habits die hard."

Levon felt as if he were going to pass out. "So, if they're the . . . the Projectionists, then what are you? I mean, you're one of them, right?"

"Right. You started to see through my scrim at the meeting tonight. A few of my fellow travelers have even started making their presence known to you in your dreams – or as members of the Bas-Relief Gang. That injury to your head opened up certain portals of perception not usually available to human beings.

"To answer your question: They are the Projectionists; I am the Usher; and *this*" – he tossed the coin in the air, caught it, then began the flip/twirl again "– is your ticket to the show; Admit One."

"I still don't under –"

"Paula. You were right about her not being dead. Glitches in the film, Levon; an electron on a TV screen that landed where it shouldn't have at a specific moment. Maybe in one possible world the two of you were meant to be crushed and killed in that accident, but not this world. It happens. The Projectionists can't see everything all the time, despite the astonishing abilities they possess.

"Is this getting through to you, pal? *It wasn't supposed to happen.* But in the microsecond that it *did* occur there wasn't time to grab both of you, so one of you – totally at random – was . . . *edited* from the scene.

"And now we're going to put together what you might call the 'Director's Cut' of how your reality should have been, with all possibilities fulfilled." He held out the coin. "You're miserable, my friend; you'll never be happy here, not without her. You don't belong here anymore."

"I, uh . . . I'm finding all of this a little hard to swallow without benefit of Castor Oil."

"What if I were to tell you that you've already started to slip over into another world?"

"I'd say you've had one beer too many."

"Really?" Hunter smiled a conspirator's smile: "Where are your crutches, Levon? For that matter, where's that oh-so-stylin' leg-brace you usually sport?"

Levon stared at his two straight, normal-looking and -feeling legs in utter astonishment.

"Oh, yeah, *now* he's getting the Big Picture." Hunter laughed. "That was a Summer Olympics-worthy jump you took off the landing earlier; I'm surprised it didn't occur to you then – but, let's face it, subtlety is often lost on you. I seem to have lost my train of thought – making light of handicaps does that to me, a flaw, I know, but we're not here to talk about my dreadful personality problems –"

" . . . something about the coin?" prompted Levon.

"Ah, yes, the coin." He held it out. "Go on, take the coin."

"Do I have to keep it moving like that?"

Hunter shook his head. "No, that was my job. As long as the coin remains in motion, the Possible World you belong in remains nearby. Once you take this in your hand, the theater is open, and therein waits the Possible World she has waiting for you – for *both* of you."

Levon wiped the sweat from his face, pulled in a deep breath, and took the coin from Hunter's hand.

The world proceeded backward, forward, downward, sideways.

He drove that night/did not drive.

They took that road/did not take it.

He saw himself crushed/thrown free and alive.

He proposed to Paula/never met her.

He killed himself because of his grief with a shotgun.

He watched himself blow his head off.

There was a glitch in the film, and the world became another world looking into another world that shifted and changed and faded into shadows to be replaced by another, firmer possible world. There were children laughing, playing, growing old, dying, turning to ashes, blowing away with the snow; there were trees growing, toppling, rotting, turning to ashes, blowing away; mountains rose and crumbled before his eyes, and with them races of peoples and creatures so fantastic he nearly wept at the sight. He was here in his home, an old and bitter man, broken by grief. He also stood across from this old man, young and alive and bright-eyed at the Possibilities; the two of them met each other in the middle of the room, whispered, "Paula," then became one, grew even younger, lost his beard, became shrunken and pink-cheeked, an infant vanishing back into the womb of its mother who spun back into time and vanished.

He thought he would be lost here forever, shifting, turning, rising, falling, becoming old and young at once, a babe and an invalid, longing for her touch, her voice, her laugh, then he felt Hunter's hand grab his shoulders and shake him and –

– and he was rooted firmly in the moment, *this* moment, the one he knew well even though he'd not chosen it.

"It's time, Levon. For a few more moments, this World, the World-Now, is frozen for you. It's time for you to step into the frame of the next movie. Paula's there – hell, she sent an escort for you." He slapped Levon's back. "Go on, do the Big Boogie."

"What about you?"

"I'll see you there, just like here and in all the other Possible Worlds. I get around a lot; many, *many* Frequent Flyer miles."

Levon gestured at Tiresias. "And Tie?"

"Take him along. It's all the same to him." He placed the mouse on Levon's shoulder and – without Levon even being aware of it – guided him out the back door into the snow-covered yard where the creature with the red balloon waited.

The falling snow seemed to have frozen in place before touching the Earth, just as the stars and moon and wind.

The creature came forward and offered Levon its hand.

He took it. The touch of its flesh summoned up the ghost of Paula's fingertips brushing against his palm.

Tiresias, his furry fellow traveler, on his shoulder, the coin gripped firmly in his hand, Levon allowed himself to be led away into the ice-sheened cluster of trees, breathless with the thought that she would soon be by his side again.

And soon, there in another winter, far away under another sky, she held her lover's hand and smiled her smile of a thousand secret flames.

And later, there in another summer, under a harsher sky, two mangled bodies were cut from the wreckage of car that had been flattened against a mountainside.

And there, in a house like a lot of other houses, on a street like a lot of other streets, a music box, until recently long-silent, started playing "The Long and Winding Road."

There was no one there to hear it, save for the memory of one brown mouse, sitting in a cage; but it, too, was fading into a place where it really belonged.

So it was that night(s) that the face of heaven was made so fine that all the world(s) fell in love with the stars.

Elsewhere, a Projectionist smiled, pleased that this particular sequence had been saved in the editing room.

At Eternity's Gate

"... true creativity demands some measure of enjoyment be subtracted from life."
– Herman Hesse, *Gertrude*

– *So, my love: How would you begin telling the story of your – of our life?*

– Who would believe it?

– I would. Tell me. Please?

– As you wish: There once was a young woman who woke one day to find that she'd been given the power to journey between this world and another. Does it sound like a splendid gift? Then consider this: She could control neither where *she would go or* when.

Do you like the way it begins?

– I do. Now, the rest, if you will.

– I will, my love, I will. Anything you ask of me ...

Lucinda turned her wheelchair away from the painting, adjusted her belly-bag, and decided that sadness was the color of rain. She knew that rain had a color – hidden though it was – for she had spent many hours studying it from behind her hospice window: Rain and sadness were the same pale shade, for she saw that color every time before one of her seizures. She'd been having so many damned seizures lately –

– boosted from her body, her thin flesh shed by her shadow, floating down that hazy corridor surrounded by faces with unreadable expressions –

– and none of the doctors could tell her why.

No wonder, though: She doubted the seizures had any rational – let alone medical – explanation.

She looked over her shoulder at the painting, realized she was too tired to continue working on it today, then leaned back her head and closed her eyes.

"I'm guessing that's your subtle way of telling me that you're finished for today?" said Jordan, the volunteer art instructor.

"I'm tired and my bag's almost full."

"Do you want me to call a nurse?"

Lucinda shook her head, forcing back the liquid numbness trying to envelope her torso – the first warning sign of an oncoming seizure. She often wondered if she wasn't subconsciously going through the Kübler-Ross final stages of death and her body was accepting what her mind didn't want to think about.

Jordan came over to her chair. "Are you sure you don't want me to –"

"No. The nurse'd only give me a shot – not that I mind. Sometimes, even when I'm not in all that much pain, I ask for one, just so I can sit very still and feel the drugs blossom inside. It's like your first cool drink on a really hot day, an ice-bird in the center of your body spreading its wings wide." She laughed. "All of which probably means I'm a junkie by now, but . . . what the hell, you know?" She opened her eyes and saw

Jordan standing in front of the painting.

"This is really quite splendid," he said. "You've come a long way in a very short time. I feel like I might have actually taught you something."

"You have, you know that. Fishing for a compliment, are we?"

He smiled at her, a perfect boyish smile from the hairy face of a bear. He seemed so much larger and more powerful today; he filled the room.

The numbness spread upward into her skull. Everything was slowing down. The darkspace opened up to her, revealing the pinpoints of light hidden behind the pale scrim of the rain. She felt weightless and freed and very much afraid.

" . . . ohgod . . ."

Jordan was next to her, taking her hand. "What is it? Is it happening again?"

" . . . yes. I d-don't want –"

But she was no longer there.

She was outside of herself, her flesh, twisting within the –

– the pinpoints that tumbled toward her, each one becoming a face that sped past with astonishing momentum, leaving only emptiness and longing in their wake, the last of them becoming a sphere as it approached her, folding in on itself until it was the very absence of space; then it flashed, an eye winking, blossoming and segmenting into a maelstrom of kaleidoscopic images: A ramshackle windmill, a group of miners emerging from the pits, a dusty country road, a field of sunflowers, boats in a harbor, a billiards room that remained before her gaze, expanding, solidifying, emitting sounds, vibrations, scents of wine and smoke and fresh-baked bread and sweat . . .

. . . She sat at a table near the entrance. The table was part of the billiards rooms, the room part of a tavern, and the tavern was overflowing with people, some festive and gay, others pensive and melancholy. Smoke drifted past her face in thin, spicy wisps. The music was muffled and somewhat discordant but appealing, nonetheless. More scents came to her: Coal dust and drying mud, hot beef and gravy, dying flowers and damp wood. She liked it very much.

Across the room two men were sitting at a scarred oak table, an opened bottle of wine between them. One of them, a great bull of a man who reminded her too much of Jordan, was laughing boisterously while his companion sat intensely – almost deathly – still, glowering with narrowed eyes and chin pressed down against his collar. He wore a tattered, wide-brimmed hat of woven straw; his beard was scraggly and auburn, his eyes bloodshot and beguiling. After a moment, he raised his head and spoke to the bull.

"I should have known better than to tell you about it, Paul. I despise you when you get this way. Everything has to amuse you or you don't want to hear about it."

"Ah, my dear friend – if only you would *listen* to yourself when you these moods come on you!"

"I find I can still recognize my own voice, thank you."

The bull named Paul leaned onto the table. "But if you could hear yourself – it isn't so much what you say, it's how you say it. Your words are often more colorful than your paintings." He sat back, brushed some hair out of his eyes, and launched into an overripe imitation. "'I tell you *it follows me!* I hear their *keening,* I see their *faces!* And I float there, trapped, frightened –'" he dramatically placed his hand against his forehead "' – *oh, so frightened,* so frightened and *aloooooooone!*'"

Merrymakers at nearby tables laughed, a few of them applauding in thanks for the entertainment.

"What?" said the Bull, looking at his companion.

"Did you find my performance less than satisfactory?"

"You wail like a woman in childbirth."

"I consider that a compliment."

"I thought you would understand," said the auburn man. "To feel that you are bodiless, unbound. I am more than just myself in that place, I am some idealized form of myself. I know there is a way out, you see, and I know that it's very close to me . . . I can *feel* it but I cannot get near it. And the crying, it follows me even after I waken. I go to my window, I look out, but there is no light to be seen in any of the houses, there are only those in the sky above, and I know that those lights contain the source of that soul-sick weeping, and I feel a force –"

"– you feel the force of drink, my friend," roared the Bull as he lifted the dusty wine bottle. "Perhaps a taste more of this will satisfactorily deafen you. If not, I can at least promise that enough of it will leave your soul to drunk to wander from your body while you're sleeping."

Lucinda felt her body go rigid; this was all very familiar, too much so: As if she had heard the echo of a sound that hadn't yet been made.

The auburn man grew suddenly furious at the Bull's words, and with a violent swing of his arm flung the wine bottle to the floor. "Isn't it enough that you perpetually mock what we do, you and I? You wear your hypocrisy like a priest donning his robes for mass. When the nobility dangle their wealth in front of your face like a scrap of meat at the lips of a starving dog, you loudly proclaim that there's such divine, moral, ethereal passion at the heart of your work – 'It is the soul in conflict with itself that is the most important thing of all' – yet you feel no remorse when you strike away the hand of a beggar in the street. How can you do that? Tell me. Make me understand how you can profess such compassion and yet continue to deny that there *is* truly a measure of pain in the universe that is born into each of us, one that cannot be eased and follows us through every moment of our existence and perhaps even beyond? Make me understand how you can go on gorging yourself on meat and wine and sleep in a sad whore's stained bed, forever turning a blind eye to the misery of humanity when you know damned well it's in your grasp, your gift, to ease part of that misery!"

"You never were any fun once the drinking started. If you were to ask me, I think –"

"Goddamn you, Paul! How can a man so brilliant be such a filthy, arrogant shit?"

The Bull's face turned into a slab of granite. "How dare you lecture me about compassion. Christ! – how many times have I listened to you bemoan the rancor that chokes you when you think of the way your fellow men treat one another? Are you telling me that it is permissible to disdain mankind as a whole yet admire individual dignity? Or are the poet and composer the same to you as the aristocrat and anarchist – deserving of scorn until they have suffered enough that you deem them worthy of your caring? For someone who purports to be a man of the people, my friend, you have a curiously selective heart."

The auburn man's eyes seemed to slide back into his skull. "I think . . . I think. . . ." He grabbed the edge of the table, shuddering.

The Bull looked suddenly terrified. "Is it happening again?"

"Not for love . . . not for any woman's love or the love of a people . . . just . . . let me awaken once with silence surrounding me . . . just once let me not hear it!" He flung himself off the chair and into a waiter, knocking them both to the floor as he kicked and moaned and flailed his arms, a thin trickle of foam crawling from the corner of his mouth. The bull leapt to his feet as the auburn man thrashed to his knees and reached for something on the table, then all too quickly a crowd gathered around the scene, laughing, shouting, pointing –

– Lucinda could catch brief glimpses of frenzied, violent movement –

– then came a crash and the howls of laughter turned to gasps, then cries of fear and disgust. The mob quickly dispersed. A gust of cinnamon smoke drifted against her eyes as she rose to see the two men.

The bull, the man called Paul, was sitting at the table, roaring with black laughter that threatened to become a snarl through his clenched teeth and tears. The auburn man was on his feet, pressed face-first against the stone wall, pounding it with his fist, scraping flesh and blood over the stones with every blow. He clutched the left side of his head with his other hand, blood streaming from between his fingers. A rusted knife lay at his feet.

The bull rose, grabbing something small and blood-sopped from the table and flinging it at the auburn man. "Here, goddamn you: Take it! Take this proof of your bloody magnificent suffering that you value more than anything else in your pathetic life! Take it and put it on your tongue and taste it and swallow it and gag on it!" He slammed his chair into the wall, splintering it into kindling, then stormed out the tavern door. The auburn man sank down, trying to pick up the severed lobe with trembling and blood-slick hands. After a moment he snapped his gaze up to Lucinda's face.

She had never seen such haunted, haunting eyes.

"Did you understand?" he whimpered. "Did you?"

She could find no words. She knelt beside him, took

the earlobe from the floor, and gently placed it in his hands.

His fingers closed around her wrist. Lucinda touched his cheek, feeling an affinity for him that she'd never experienced before.

His voice was the whisper of a child lost in the darkness: "Have you ever felt it?"

She wanted to answer him, to say that she had, she was, but the numbness had returned and was seducing her, drawing her back through the darkspace and into the pale shade of rain; a surge of suffocating pressure.

The auburn man spoke her name, his image dwindling.

"Lucinda?"

She reached toward him but he was mist.

"Lucinda?"

Shaking her by the shoulders. Her head lolled to the side and she opened her eyes to see Jordan kneeling in front of her wheelchair –

– no, it was there, on the other side of the room.

She was in her bed, her head cradled by pillows, and Jordan was sitting on the edge, holding her hand. She blinked, saw the clear tube rising from the bandage on her arm, snaking up to an IV drip. She drew in a short, sharp breath that filled her torso with fire. She touched her belly-bag; it was empty.

"Jordan." She felt a smile. "Is it morning already? I don't remember when I –"

He rose to his feet, stepped away, and turned her painting toward her.

"Jordan? What are you – ?"

The words caught in her throat.

The painting was finished. She could clearly see that it conveyed everything she had intended; the gulls seemed to shimmer as they soared toward the morning sun, the sands had a life all their own, shifting and scattering and drowning under the foaming force of the ocean.

Not looking at Jordan, she whispered, "How . . . how long have you been here?"

"A day. A day and a half. You don't remember?"

She shook her head. "All I can remember is feeling the numbness right before the seizure, hearing the sounds of someone crying . . . a lot of people crying, then. . . ."

She closed her eyes and breathed slowly, steadily, her mind grasping at the remnants of images, finally focusing on that of a scarred tabletop –

– and she remembered what had happened to her beyond the darkspace.

Opening her eyes, she asked Jordan what he had seen and heard.

"You had a seizure. I called for the nurse. We took you from the chair and put you in bed. I wanted to stay but a doctor came in and ordered me to leave. I came back early the next morning. They told me that you were fine, that you were conscious and were working on a painting. I came in and found you. . . ." He gestured toward the easel. There was a deep, drying stain on the carpet. Lucinda blanched; once before, after she'd first arrived at the hospice, she'd tried to stand while her belly-bag was full, only to have it burst and slop down her legs, filling the air with a stench so overpowering and rancid it caused her to faint. Standing was, had always been, would probably always be, a nearly insurmountable task, requiring reserves of strength she couldn't sustain. So weak, so damned weak and sickly ever since childhood. She had firmly believed that she wouldn't live to see seventeen, let alone twenty-eight. She used to imagine herself just snapping off one night, doing a Granny Weatherall and click-ing out, not living long enough to watch her life grind to a halt in a series of repulsive, sputtering little agonies. She never thought her last days, weeks, months – however the hell long it was – would be spent like this. She looked at her tutor and felt a pressure in her throat.

"How did I – ?"

Jordan placed his hand against her cheek. His touch was satin. "You spoke almost constantly. In French. Why didn't you ever tell me that you spoke my native language?"

"I . . . I don't. I flunked French in high school. I picked up one or two phrases, a half-dozen words, but –"

Jordan shook his head. "No, this wasn't textbook French spoken in a mock accent. You spoke it as fluently as if you'd been speaking it all your life. You used slangs and idioms I haven't heard since I was a boy in Asnieres."

"But . . . how?"

He only stared at her.

"I was standing? Moving?"

He gave a slow nod of his head. Lucinda suddenly felt exposed and vulnerable and angry for that vulnerability but leaned toward him anyway, burying her face in his chest, feeling his massive arms enfold her like they would a frightened child, her fear and confusion temporarily held at bay as she filled herself with the scents of his body. The smell of a man, she thought. The nearness. She felt something trickle into her belly-bag, and once again silently railed against nothing and everything for her condition, her heart aching at the memory of the auburn man clutching his bleeding head.

Jordan pulled back and cupped her face in his hands, staring into her eyes. "The man you spoke of, the 'auburn man.' Would you know his face if you saw it again?"

She thought of his eyes that haunted, and whispered, "Yes." Jordan smiled at her, the same smile he gave her when a painting was going well. She adored that smile.

He turned away from her and picked up a large book from the bedside table, a thick, heavy volume whose pages held photographs of various artists and their work.

As he flipped past pictures and biographies of Frans Hals and Michelangelo and El Greco he said, "It never occurred to me that I should educate you about various styles or artists. It was so rare to find someone like you, someone who was born with a natural aptitude and had never been exposed to fine art in any way. The minute I saw your work I knew that yours was a genuine talent. All my life I've waited for a student like you. I –" He sighed. "I'm sorry. I was going to make a point with that but I seem to have lost track."

"You get used to it."

He looked up. "Do you know how much I hate it that you're so sick? Do you have any idea how –"

"– please don't. Please."

He reluctantly returned his attention to the volume on his lap.

Lucinda felt weaker than ever, and wondered if the seizures would ever stop – or, at the very least, lessen in their intensity, fade away as Jordan was now, as if being swallowed by a fog.

Jordan turned the book toward her, one beefy finger resting next to a portrait. "Is this the auburn man?"

"How did you know?"

"Is it him?" His voice was glass.

"Yes." She felt her body tugged forward as the fog cleared and the darkspace emerged from behind, creeping toward her, its silvery pinpoints blinking.

"*Arles*," he whispered. "You were with Vincent at Arles. Dear God."

She wanted to hold his hand but he was now an intangible and she was cascading on the pale shade of rain down a hazy corridor, flying past faces and strange dream-figures – one of them a lithe female figure with the head of a black horse, ears erect, neck arched, vapor jetting from its nostrils, and she thought she should know this figure, this strange creature, this thing of wonder – then she was drifting, finally feeling her feet touch the cold marble floor of a long hall. She walked haltingly until she arrived at the section where he waited for her. Standing at the doorway she could smell the stench of human waste, could hear the wretched outcries of the other patients. She moved through the doorway, tripping over an emaciated woman lying naked on the floor, shuddering violently, the soles of her mangled feet smacking against the wall with a moist, raw sound. Lucinda stepped aside, staring in muted horror as vomit dribbled from the woman's mouth, then flew out and up in a sickening spray as she began to thrash about, clawing at her throat.

The patients were roaming everywhere; staring, singing to themselves, weeping. Their voices rose to the ceiling, the echoes expanding, touching, coalescing, then crashing down on her head; it was the sound of a million babies doused with gasoline and set aflame, the cry of a million broken-hearted men shrieking their anguish into the black, uncaring night, the keening of countless ages of affliction all come to rest in this spot, at this moment, searing her to the core.

She felt disgusted by it, sorry for it, yet at the same time an intricate part of it all. She watched the patients slide down the clammy marble walls like flies struggling to break free of a spider's web, writhe deep inside cement bathtubs, squat in corners relieving their tortured bowels, cover their heads to protect themselves from blows delivered by invisible assailants, all of them muttering in low, hoarse, lunatic voices.

Then she saw Vincent.

He was sitting on his bed next to a large barred window, and he was sketching. Occasionally he would stop, stretch, and scratch at the bandage on the left side of his head. He watched him for several moments until he at last noticed her, smiled, and gestured for her to join him.

"What are you drawing?" she asked as she sat next to him. He pointed out the window. Down in the yard Lucinda saw other patients, these wearing flowing white gowns, walking around a large stone fountain as if it would take them elsewhere.

"Look at them," muttered Vincent. "You and I should know such contentment." He blended a shadow with his index finger, put the sketch down, and turned to her. "Everyone suffers here, be it from madness, disease, loneliness or pain, everyone suffers. We understand each other like members of the same family." He took her hands in his; his palms were rough and calloused but they felt like a rose cradled in her grasp.

"When will you leave this terrible place?"

"Soon, if I am to take Dr. Gachet for a man of his word. I will visit with Theo for a while and then, I suspect, I will go to a place I have often dreamt of retiring to."

"Where?"

"Auvers-sur-Oise. God speaks through its landscape. There is a field there I have always wanted to paint."

Lucinda moved closer, kissing him on the cheek. "May I come to be with you there?"

"Yes. I need you by my side very badly. Once I feared that all my tenderness had died with Margot, then you –" He pulled her to him. "You have given me back something of myself I thought long dead."

"I do so want to be with you. It's been two months since you came here, yet this is the first time I've been allowed to see you."

"Oh, my lovely lady, why is that so important? You must have known that I would come to find you after my release. Why come to see me in this . . . this squalor?"

"Because I know what you meant now. In my dreams I, too, see the other faces. I hear their weeping and when I wake I can spare little thought for anything else. You are not a madman, you are not possessed."

"Then, you feel it too? That sense of being . . . lost within those cries? Abandoned?"

"Yes."

He grunted, released her hands, and turned away. "All colors are ones of despair," he whispered. "Red is man's rage, yellow his lust, blue his reason and gray his conscience. Green is his spirit, shit-brown his heart, and all of the them are moving toward the same place, a place where they will unite into blackness and . . . unimaginable nothing." He wiped something from his eye, peered out into the courtyard, and began shaking.

"'Once, when I was in the Borinage, I painted the miners there, and the colors seemed so majestic when used for them. It was one of those times – all but lost now – when I felt as one with the colors. I used to think red was the color of love, after all – be it sentimental tripe or not; a rose awaiting the touch of the sun so it might fully blossom, then be plucked from its stem and held in the hands of a beautiful woman." He arched backward, gasping in harsh breaths, one hand pressing against his chest.

"But no matter how hard I try the colors come out their darkest now. And nowhere are they darker than in my dreams. It terrifies me. Not only do I feel that I have been abandoned among those weeping faces, but each time I sleep now I feel as if I'm getting closer to the moment when that unseen exit will close behind me before I can return to my body and awaken, and I will be trapped in there forever." He smiled a crooked grin. "Shall I tell you my greatest fear? The one that is always in the front of my mind, compelling everything I do? It is that I will never live long enough to paint all the pictures in my head. And do you know why? Because I have betrayed the colors, and they are punishing me by putting me in that unknowable place between the mind and soul every time I sleep. I don't want to go back, do you see? It is so . . . so lonely there."

Lucinda reached out to touch him, but before she could reach he leapt from the bed and grabbed the bars on the window.

His cry was filled with rain.

"When the day is over will you weep at the passing of the sun and all it has given you to see? Will you rejoice when the dawn arrives at all the chances it offers? Will you take the hands of a ragged one, an odd, damaged, discarded one? Will you bring them mercy and comfort, tell them that this madness and loneliness will pass?" He began pounding against the bars with an opened hand. In the distance Lucinda could hear the attendants running down the hall. She rose from the bed and once again tried to touch him – she knew she was trying because she could feel her limbs moving – yet she was suddenly outside herself, staring down, watching herself remain motionless.

Vincent began ramming his head against the bars. "No! No, you will not! You shall drink and laugh and close your eyes to all of it. You shall mock the lost and lonely ones, spit on the poor, and in that lonely place where my dreams send me there shall emerge another face twisted in pain. *YOU WILL FORGET! YOU ARE DEAF!*" The attendants fell on him, dragging him to the ground and strapping his arms behind his back. One of them tore his bandage as they dragged him down the corridor and Lucinda rose, only to be wrenched away and hurled into the darkspace, and there she saw the faces of others lost in dreams and agony, trying to find their way back to bodies long since dead and buried and rotting under the earth. Their mouths opened to release wails of misery; their eyes shed tears that became starlight pinpoints, ebbing away from her, and she lurched forward, dropping her palette and gasping for breath.

Jordan was sitting on the floor in front of her chair, drinking a glass of beer and leafing through a book, one of many that were scattered around him. His eyes were red from lack of sleep.

Then she saw her new painting.

An old, emotionally broken man, sitting in a small, weak chair, his head buried in his thin, calloused hands. The room surrounding him was bare and decrepit, its sole window looking out on a golden field and blue sky. Across from the old man she could see the traced outline, barely discernable, of another chair yet to be painted. The scene was one of breathtaking beauty and melancholy, and though the brush which had composed the scene may have been held by her hand, another's had guided it.

The colors were not applied with her usual smooth strokes but, rather, a uneasy yet oddly effective combination of her strokes fused with violent, almost frenzied slashes; the picture seemed to vibrate.

"Four days this time," said Jordan. "You refused to remain in your chair, but your bag didn't leak."

She looked down at her belly-bag and saw that it was empty. There was no discomfort now. She felt the pale shade fading, the darkspace moving farther away.

"Was I still speaking in French?"

"Yes." He stared at her. "You know who he is now, don't you?"

"Van Gogh?"

"Van Gogh." He poured a glass of water and helped her to hold it while she drank. She smiled her thanks, he covered her with a blanket, and she eased back in the wheelchair.

"It's not like a dream at all," she said. "I am there. I make a difference."

Jordan tried to smile and failed miserably. "There's a lot I need to explain to you. *Try* to explain, anyway. I'm not sure I understand some of it myself." He shook himself and took a deep breath, then pointed toward the new painting.

"This painting is based on a long-lost sketch Van Gogh did entitled *Worn Out: At Eternity's Gate.* He remarked once in a letter to his brother Theo that he couldn't begin the actual painting until he found the right color scheme. He said that if he could realize the proper balance and light composition, then he'd know what was missing from the picture. He did a preliminary version of this piece that many historians have mistakenly assumed was the finished product. He believed it might have been the fruition of all he'd been striving toward in his work."

Lucinda could not, did not want to, grasp what he was saying. "And you're telling me that this is . . . this is the way Van Gogh wanted it done?"

"Yes . . . and no. There's as much of you in this as him."

She shook her head. "How could I have –"

Jordan took hold of her hands. "Listen to me. I've been thinking back to when I was boy. When I was eight, I came down with a serious fever that lasted nearly ten days. The doctors thought I would die. During that time, whenever I fell asleep, I would have these absolutely terrifying nightmares. One night I woke up after a particularly scary one and found my father sitting at my bedside. I remember the way he stroked my hair and sang to me, the way his hands felt when he placed a cool, moist rag over my forehead . . . he was a very kind man and I miss him . . . anyway, on this night, I refused to go back to sleep.

"He told me, then, about the tunnel that our soul flies through whenever we dream, that all souls travel through this tunnel, even those of people who have died and are on their way to God. Somewhere along the way, this tunnel separates into two branches – the dead take one branch, the dreamers take another. But sometimes the dreamers and the dead get confused along the way and don't know which branch to take once they arrive at that point. A dreamer has the luxury of simply turning around and going back, but the dead have to remain there, alone and afraid, and that's what causes us to have nightmares – that fear. The lonely fear that the dead have."

"The Lady or the Tiger?" said Lucinda.

"Something like that, yes. As I grew older I developed an interest in dreams and did a great deal of reading about them. I also read about astral projection, fever-dreams, what happens to the mind of someone who is in a coma or experiencing a seizure – and, of course, near-death experiences. In almost every account I came across, the people described a long corridor, or road, or tunnel, and each saw a light at the end. I began to wonder, What if it's true? What if there is a place out there along the path of dreams where the road – the tunnel – branches, and there are countless frightened spirits – spirits of the dead – just standing there, uncertain of which way to go?"

Lucinda shook her head. "I still don't quite –"

"Let's just say, for the moment, that it is true, all

right? And let's say that, eventually, one of these spirits of the dead decides, to hell with it, and chooses a branch, only it turns out to be the wrong one. Think about it. What would you do?"

Lucinda felt a familiar ache in her chest. She tried not to think about the moment of her approaching death because it would come soon enough. "I don't know. I . . . I guess that I'd try to find my way back to the branch."

"And if you couldn't?"

She bit her lower lip. "I don't want to talk about this any longer, Jordan, please? Why are you –"

He snatched another book from the floor, opening to a previously marked page. "This is an excerpt from a letter Van Gogh sent to Theo in July of 1883. He was talking about what he experienced during his seizures. Listen to this: 'When I am at work I feel an unlimited faith in art and in its healing powers, yet I must take care that I carry that faith with me into the opaque blackness when it enfolds me, as it so often does these days. It astounds me, this *dark space,* for as it swallows me it releases me, also, and I feel weightless, as if being carried away by thousands of glittering pinpoints of light to a place where everything in this tiny universe convenes, a place where life and death meet for a while to tell each other their stories. I believe when I arrive at this place I will find the answers that have been missing in my life. Only there will I be freed to paint as I always should have, to bring my work to fruition, to perfect that one last image which has eluded me for all my days and dreams. I know such things are pure fancy, for even if it is true, I will be among the bodiless, then, the brush forever out of my reach. But I grow weary and the words on this page blur, so I leave you for now.'" He snapped the book closed and stared at Lucinda.

She swallowed, once, painfully and said, "So you think that . . . that –"

"I think that when Van Gogh died his spirit took the wrong branch. I think he was lost there until you came along. I think that during one of your seizures your soul met his in the dream branch and he recognized you for what you are. He knows that he is dead and that you –" His voice cracked on the next two words. "– are dying, so he's . . . I think he saw in you his chance to come back into this life long enough to bring his work 'to fruition.'"

Jordan's eyes filled with wonder. "All their lives artists wonder where it comes from, their gift for creation. You've said yourself, and I've experienced it too, that there are times when a work seems to be creating itself and is only using you as a conduit. Look at the painting. It's your style, yes, but it's evolving at an incredible rate."

"But –"

"Don't you see? This painting was to be Van Gogh's summation of all he'd done, but he never figured out what was missing from the sketch. He's finishing the work not only through you, but with you, as well. Your two styles are merging into one."

He dropped the book onto the floor.

It took a moment for the full impact of everything to hit her; then Lucinda began shaking. "But . . . why me?"

"Because you share his loneliness, his pain and isolation." Jordan knelt down and held both her hands.

"Tell me, the first time in the tavern, is that when he mutilated himself?"

"Yes."

"Gauguin was there, that's right. October of 1888. And the second time?"

"An asylum."

"That would be Saint-Remy. May, 1889."

"Why are the dates so important?"

"Because after Van Gogh left the asylum he retired to –"

"Auvers-sur-Oise?"

"He told you?"

"Yes. I promised to meet him there." The blood drained from Jordan's face.

"What is it?" asked Lucinda.

Jordan shook his head. "I don't want –"

"Say it."

His eyes met hers. "If this is what's happening, if all he wants is for the two of you to finish this last piece, then why are you going back into his past? Why is he sharing only certain moments with you? There's no need."

"Why does that scare you?"

"Because on July 27th, 1890, Van Gogh shot himself in the chest in the field outside Auvers. He died thirty-six hours later."

Lucinda was transfixed. "He mentioned a Margot?"

"A neighbor in Holland when he lived there in 1884. Margot Begemann. He loved her dearly, but both families were bitterly opposed to their love. She committed suicide after several failed attempts. It was shortly after that he began his 'crises' periods. That was when those violent slashes became predominate in his work."

"His 'crises' . . . were those his own seizures? Like mine?"

"I'm almost positive."

"But why are my seizures so . . . so unrelenting now?"

"Because whatever it is he needs to do through you needs to be done soon. When was the last time you looked at a calendar?"

"I don't remember."

"Today is July 27th."

". . . and the painting still isn't finished? Is that what scares you?"

Jordan was a statue. "No. What scares me is the thought that goes through my mind when I try to see this from his point of view. I love life, and I love my work. I think I would be willing to do anything to ensure that I could keep on creating for as long as possible."

Lucinda rubbed her eyes and exhaled impatiently. "I wish you'd tell me what it is that's –"

"What if he's decided that a few more months of life, even life in a sick body, is better than staying where he is now? What if he's taking you back into his past, to places you have never seen before, in order to – Christ, I can't believe I'd think this of him – in order to leave you there so he might use your –"

"Whoa," said Lucinda, holding up her hands. "Stop right there. Now, I will admit that this is all quite . . . extraordinary. We both know that something is definitely going on here, but when you start saying that Vincent is trying to trick me out of my body so he can move in for a little while, it's crossing the line into something too weird, Jordan. Do you understand? I'm not totally naïve about people. I think I'm perceptive enough to know when someone has a hidden agenda and I truly don't think he does." She was shaking. "I really can't talk about this anymore, at least not right now. I don't feel well, I really don't, and I'm sick of it: Okay? I know that I insisted you tell me what was bothering you but now I'm sorry I did because you're right, it's kind of scary, so can we just drop it for a little bit? Can we just stay here and enjoy each other's company?"

He leaned forward and kissed her; gently, warmly, compassionately.

Lucinda felt her bowels shift. A thick, wet gurgle filled the air as something leaked into her belly-bag. She looked away from Jordan. "You must find me repulsive."

"Far from it. Even the colors of autumn cannot compare to your eyes. Oh, Lord – I can't believe I said something that corny."

Lucinda began weeping. The smell from her belly-bag reached her, causing her to cough and weep all the more; for all the days of her childhood spent alone in her room, a sketchbook her only companion; for all the times she'd sat listening to the other children playing outside her window, laughing and shouting as they rode their bicycles and played sandlot baseball and argued whose turn it was next on the swing; for all the moments when she looked up from her work long enough to realize that she would never be a part of it, and there was no self-pity in these tears, only an aching resignation which was as much a part of her as her flesh and shadow. Just to have one of those days back, to be a normal healthy child for just a few hours, to have known the joy of jumping into a pile of leaves, a mud fight, a quick, silly game of hide-and-go-seek.

Then the regret blossomed and matured, meeting her at this point in time, making her wish that she were sitting here a whole and desirable woman, one who didn't rage against the frailty that entrapped her, one who didn't have to resort to the humiliating recourse of tears in order to grapple with the cold equations that equaled her reality, a woman who –

– she took a deep breath and began to calm herself. She felt Jordan release the brakes on her wheelchair and begin pushing her toward her dresser. In the mirror her hair looked tangled and lifeless, not the bright, glowing stream of copper that it was when she was freshly showered.

Jordan smiled at her reflection. "I can see why he is so taken by you. If I were in his position, I wouldn't hesitate to travel across time for you."

She wiped her eyes.

Jordan picked up a brush and ran it through her hair. "See?" he whispered. "A countess is born."

"You may kiss my ring, good sir."

Jordan laughed his roaring Frenchman's laugh, filling her with a sense of need and being needed; a sense of place and comfort.

Then he turned her chair around and kissed her again.

She felt herself grow warm; she could barely contain the excitement his touch brought to her. She gently put her arms around his neck.

"I have been alone most of my life," he said, never looking away from her eyes. "Children mocked me because of my size, my face . . . I've had little need for any companionship aside from the easel, canvas, and brush. After I turned forty I realized that something was absent from my life, so I volunteered to give free art classes at various grade schools and hospitals and . . . well, that's how I came to be here. I look at you and feel the heat of a thousand secret flames. Your breath is a song to me, whispering promise. I feel as if the arc of my life has been pointing toward this moment for all of my days. And sometimes, when the light comes in through the window and you turn to look at it, your eyes sparkle and I imagine I know what God must have felt like the first time He gazed upon the creation that was woman . . . or maybe I'm just full of shit and you happen to be beautiful but can't see it and I've been in love with you for a long time."

Lucinda pulled him to her and kissed him once again. Then, suddenly, as she lay her head against his shoulder, the effects of the last several days draped over her; she felt the sweat, the pain, the time.

"Jordan, I. .I'd like to take a bath but I don't . . . oh God, this is harder than I thought it would be. I don't want you to call the nurse to help. I hope you don't –"

He picked her up out of the wheelchair and carried her into the bathroom.

As he gently bathed her body he took great care not to jostle her belly-bag. "I want to tell you one more thing," he whispered. The water seeping from the cloth in his hands massaged her with warmth, easing the strain. "I know, now, that I was meant to be here for you. Shhh – don't say anything, just listen. It used to be, when I told someone the story of my life, it would stop there. But since I've met you . . ." She closed her eyes and Jordan kissed her wet hair and placed another warm, soaked cloth over her face. "Since I've known you, I have told you the story of my life, and you've asked to hear it again . . . and I find, now, that when I tell it over, it's no longer my story. It's *ours*, and I will protect that with sword and shield." The diamond droplets of water trickled down her cheek, glided over her chin, slipped down her neck, and slid a moist path between her breasts; then his hand was there, the soapy washcloth rubbing gentle circular patterns, moist and creamy, lilac-scented, and she stretched, arching her back, sighing as the washcloth dropped away and his lips began trailing down her neck, pausing at her shoulder, then to the slope of her breast, then he delicately cupped one breast in his hand, his thumb stroking her nipple until it became firm. His lips covered her nipple, drawing it into his mouth meekly yet hungrily, and she closed her eyes all the tighter, hearing a low growl rise from deep in her throat, emerging as a sigh, and the slowly drifting lights behind her closed lids separated, shimmering in rhythm with the spasms below her waist, becoming thousands of bright pinpoints that seemed to surge from somewhere in her center as she reached out and clutched the back of his head, guiding his wonderful lips to her other breast, feeling him take the nipple in his mouth as the fire and lights within her intensified, caressing her, moving her, rocking her, tickling, rolling, arching her toward him, and she felt the softness of the bed beneath, the satiny brush of the sheets, his firmness inside her, pulling back teasingly before plunging in again, and she held him close, pulled him into her until she thought he was buried inside up to her throat as she shuddered and pulled her legs against his pressing hips, digging her fingers into his shoulders, forcing him deeper as she threw her head back and cried out –

– then he kissed her neck again, whispered something she didn't understand, and moved away.

She blinked, rolled over on the bed, and saw Vincent staring out the window. His face glistened from the lights in the street below. The echoes of music and laughter drifted into the room on an intoxicating midnight breeze.

He seemed so weary, so worn-out.

"What is troubling you?"

"I am so very happy that you are here with me," he said.

She rose from the bed and quickly dressed, then joined him by the window, feeling somehow detached from everything, as if part of her had remained trapped in the dream branch.

"Something is wrong," she whispered.

"Did you know that you talk in your sleep?"

"What do I say?"

"You talk of strange people and places. Who is this Jordan you keep mentioning?"

A great jolt tore through her, pulling her out of herself, allowing her to hover above the scene for an instant, then spiraling her back down to Vincent's side.

She felt dizzy and disoriented. Van Gogh put a hand on her shoulder. "Are you all right, my dear?"

"Yes, fine . . . thank you." Something felt . . . felt –

– then Van Gogh was leading her toward the door. "Come. Walk with me. I want to show the field. I want you to be with me at . . . I want you there. I need for you to be there with me. I've a gift I wish for you to take."

She thought she detected the echo of someone else calling her name.

"You should sleep," she said. "You've not been well and –" He touched her lips, and she was silent.

"I mourn for many things, my love. I mourn for the damage we have done to our souls, I mourn for the starving and the lonely and the madness in us all, the loss of our wonder . . . but when all is said and done, no notice is taken. I cry and lament, I rage at friends and strangers, I do myself harm, but in the end, as ever always, I go out at night to paint the stars."

Once again Lucinda was jolted from her body, and as she hovered this time she saw the many darkspace faces clearly, though she recognized none. Looking down she saw not Van Gogh but Jordan, holding her in his arms, his words a dim echo in the thick air.

". . . he can't have you, I won't let . . ."

Then she was plunging down to a field upon which the moon and stars cast an ethereal glow. She glimpsed the hunched shadow of man, heard the great, unmistakable crack of gunfire, and cried out.

The darkspace came to her again, but this time only one face passed her, a face she recognized, but then there was nothing but the wind, wrapping its arms around her. She began walking through the field. Her foot brushed against something. She knelt to pick it up.

A smoking pistol.

A great pain took possession of her core. Slipping the pistol into her pocket, she stumbled out of the field and through the mazelike streets back to Van Gogh's flat. She opened the door and crossed to the bed, then lay down, the pain finding fiery focus in her chest.

She closed her eyes and saw windmills and dim pool halls, noble miners marching out of caves, shimmering trees under starry skies, an old man sitting in his chair, hunched over, his face buried in his hands –

– and realized that something about this last image was different from the painting at the hospice. Before she could discern what it was, someone jostled her arm.

She opened her eyes and saw a stranger looking down at her. His eyes were gray and his face deeply lined with worry. He brushed some hair out of her eyes and dabbed at her forehead with a cool, wet cloth.

"Shh," said the stranger. "Do not try to speak. The doctor will be here soon." She looked slowly around; she was still in Vincent's flat. Something was leaking from her belly-bag –

– no, not her bag, not at all, so what –

– she looked down.

The center of her chest was pulp; bleeding and painful.

"What is . . . who are . . ."

The voice issuing from her throat wasn't hers but she recognized it, nonetheless.

"Don't you recognize me, brother?" whispered the stranger, wiping tears from his eyes. "It's me, Theo. Please, Vincent, say that you know me."

Then she knew.

Jordan had been right.

And, quietly, she resigned herself to die in Vincent's place.

"No one will ever know," she whispered. "And if

they did, no one would ever believe it." She wondered how long it would take before Jordan realized that the person living in her body and speaking in her voice was not her, but Van Gogh. She wondered what they would do, how they would react, whether or not they would dare to tell anyone.

Theo's face became a fleshy blur as he picked up a pillow.

"I wish I could die now," she said in Van Gogh's voice.

And was answered somewhere in the darkness by an echo: *Only a moment longer, my love, my friend. All I wished was just a few moments alone with the image, nothing more, and then I shall give to you all the pictures in my head that I never lived to paint. Forgive me for my selfishness but I had to see for myself what you have done with my sketch, how you took the base and built upon the image I was no longer worthy to express. I am sorry for frightening you, but I will leave you now – but know this one last thing to be true: I treasure you.*

Don't you know that I would never abandon you to darkness?

There is no image worth the price of a soul.

Then the pillow was pressing against her face, pushing down, cutting off her breath. She became aware of the darkspace, the tunnel, the faces and bright pinpoints, and her heart ached for the loss of Jordan and what time might have remained for them, and suddenly, as she felt herself slipping away one last time, she wanted to be with him again, not here, not dying in Vincent's place, and she raged against the darkspace, choking, her mind screaming out Jordan's name as her hands began flailing against the stone-heavy pillow –

– *remember me to your Jordan, my love* –

– which suddenly was pulled away.

Her chest hitched, and she coughed, blinking her

eyes against the light.

Two beefy hands cupped her face.

"Lucinda?"

She opened her eyes and saw him leaning over her.

"Jordan?"

He pulled her into him, embracing her and weeping. "I'm sorry," he said, throwing the pillow aside. "I could think of no other way to force him to leave, to make you return to me. I would have hated living from this moment on without you."

As she lay her head against his shoulder, whispering, "We were wrong about Vincent, my love," she saw the painting, complete at last.

The old man was no longer alone.

Across from him sat an elegant, aged woman who was looking at him and laughing. She was the ghost of an errant wish – that a woman might never lose the radiance which crossed her features when a suitor came to call, never see her beauty dissolve little by little in the unflattering light of each dawn, and never know a day when the scent of roses from an admirer did not fill her rooms. She was every night you sat alone and lonely, wishing for the warm hand of a lover to hold in your own as autumn dimmed into winter and youth turned to look at you over its shoulder and whisper farewell: all this was in her face, accentuated by a benevolent resignation that told you she was happy, here in this room with this hunched old man who, Lucinda could now see, was not weeping into his hands but, rather, laughing at a joke just told to him by the woman. The scene shone with quiet joy, well-earned repose, and a sense of home; at the last, a home finally found.

As she wrapped her arms around Jordan, she smiled, part of her mind wishing Vincent peace.

I will paint the stars in your memory, she thought.

Outside, it began to sprinkle, and Lucinda decided that she'd had it all wrong; after so many years of staring out countless lonely windows, after so many years of daydreaming among the raindrops that whispered against the glass, after so many years of wishing for a home and the tenderness of a loved one, she finally realized that it wasn't the color of sadness, after all . . .

Rain was very, very pretty.

Palimpsest Day

"As far as the past goes, my philosophy's always been: Never look back – something might be gaining on you."

– Robert Mitchum, on
The Tonight Show With Johnny Carson.

1. Teach Your Children

Toward the end of her life my mother developed a fervent belief in reincarnation. During our last conversation in the hospital (in which she confessed something that stunned me), she asked about the state of my life, nodded her head in sympathy when I told her I was having trouble dealing with my sister's care and had briefly considered putting her in a group home, and then said the single most amazing thing that she'd ever said to me: "You know what you need to do, hon? You need to walk out of here today and live your life as if you were already living it for the second time and as if you had acted the first time as wrongly as you are about to act now."

I remember the way the sheets formed a perfect outline of her cancer-ravaged body. I imagined that the mattress had adapted itself into the shape of her underside. Then an odd image crossed my mind: Mom's body had been taken away, but the sheets still held the impression of Mom-front, while the bed had the shape of Mom-back, and in between was this space cast in her form where sheets and bed thought she still existed.

It wasn't until later – weeks after her funeral, she and my father side by side in Cedar Hill Cemetery – that the full weight of her words hit me. She was trying to tell me that it was possible for a person to turn the present into the past, and that the past may yet be changed and amended. Each moment of which life consists is itself dying as it's being experienced, and will never recur (or, at least, it's not *supposed* to) – but it's that very transitoriness that challenges us to make the best possible use of each moment. *Live your life as if you were already living for the second time and as if you had acted the first time as wrongly as you are about to act now.*

Those words, and their unspoken subtext that second chances exist simultaneously within *first* ones, were my mother's last and greatest gift to me, a blessing to live without fear of further regrets.

Then Laura came back into my life and I discovered they were a warning, as well.

Electrons would have to be 10^{22} times more massive for the electric and gravitational pull between two of them to be equal. To produce such a heavy particle would take 10^{19} gigaelectron volts (GeV) of energy, a quantity know as Planck *energy. Coupled with this is the Planck length, a tiny* 10^{35} *meter. Quantum physicists now believe, with the advent of such miracles as the Large Hadron Collider, it might very well be possible to circumvent Heisenberg's Uncertainty Principle and measure space-time's most staggeringly small quantities without collapsing the wave/particle duality. Using Planck time –* 10^{45} *of a second – it's theoretically possible to measure a spacetime quantity as small as* 1.62×10^{33}. *The trick is to make sure it goes smoothly, because at that size, space and time come apart.*

Lately, I've been thinking about this. A lot. If something were to happen during that period of measurement, then something else, and if the two events were separated by only 10^{45} *of a second, then when the measuring is over it would be impossible to tell which came first, space or time.*

So what would happen then? And how would we know?

2. Lucky in the Morning/Roll with the Changes

There was a time when Ayds (spelled with a "y") was a popular and surprisingly tasty dietetic candy that came in plastic bags containing individually-wrapped pieces. You could easily find it on store shelves right alongside Sweathog coffee mugs, *The Wit and Wisdom of Archie Bunker,* Kiss comic books, and *Chico and the Man* lunch boxes. The manufacturer stopped making it when the Center for Disease Control concluded that the so-called "gay flu" was a much more virulent and less discriminating strain of virus than was first suspected, because AIDS (definitely *not* spelled with a "y") was spreading beyond the partners of the nameless "Mr. X" and into the general population. The bags that were still on store shelves were slowly and quietly recalled, and by July, 1982, it was nowhere to be found.

On the morning when all of this shifted into a higher gear – some twenty-plus years after Ayds had ceased being manufactured – I awoke to find three pounds of it in my refrigerator.

It happened like this:

The previous night I was awakened by Blair bumping around in the hallway. My sister tends to get up at least once every night to use the bathroom, but there's a catch: She likes to lie in bed and wait until the last possible moment before making a beeline for the john, just to see if she'll make it in time. She enjoys the hell out of it . . . probably because she's not the one who has to deal with the various . . . let's call it *paraphernalia* that's left around when she loses her little game.

Because she'd lately started bumping into things, I put a small night light in the hall which I turn on before going to bed. I heard her stumbling around and starting to cry, so I cleared my throat and called out, "Wait for your eyes to adjust to the light, honey."

When there was no further noise, I took it to mean she'd found her way all right, and went back to sleep.

I woke up around eight-thirty a.m., got dressed, and was starting downstairs when my foot caught on something at the edge of the landing and I almost fell.

There used to be a section of old carpeting at the top of the stairs that had come loose and was sticking up just enough that you could easily slide your foot right under it if you weren't paying attention, lose your balance, and fall face-first down the stairs.

I'd removed the carpeting from the house about a

year ago, after both Blair and myself had experienced one near-miss too many. (The house was now polished hardwood floors top to bottom, courtesy of Yours Truly's efforts.) I looked down at my feet and saw absolutely nothing that could have tripped me, but I swear it felt as if I'd caught my foot in that old piece of carpeting.

"Sharp as ever, aren't you, Danny?" I whispered to myself. I went downstairs, made a pot of coffee, then went outside to retrieve the paper.

I was just turning to go back inside when a voice shouted, "Looks like your paint job ain't holding up so good!"

I turned and saw our neighbor from across the street, Mr. Finney, working in his garden. I waved to him and he rose from his rhododendrons and started walking over. I met him at the curb and we shook hands.

"What's wrong with the paint job?" I asked. I had painted the house about a year ago with an all-weather brand that cost more than I could probably afford, but I'd figured it was better to shell out the cash once and not have to worry about it again for several years.

"Take a look," he said, and pointed.

Running from the eaves of the house to nearly the floor of the front porch was a streak of white paint. Mr. Finney accompanied me as I went for a closer look. Last year, when I'd spent the better part of a week painting the house myself, Mr. Finney – a seventy-eight year-old widower who likes to keep himself occupied with gardening and neighborhood gossip – had loaned me his extension ladder to save me the cost of renting one. Then he spent several hours each afternoon sitting on his porch watching me work, always offering a cold glass of lemonade when I finished for the day.

"That's a damn shame," he said. "I mean, after you did all that work."

The streak was about the width of a standard seven-inch paint brush, and formed a nice straight line down the front of the house.

"How long's it been this way?" he asked.

"I don't know. I mean, it sure as hell wasn't this way yesterday. I'd've noticed something like this when I came home."

"You sure about that?"

"Yes. Look at it!"

Finney shook his head. "Maybe we got ourselves some practical jokers running around the neighborhood."

"I don't think so." I pointed up toward the eaves. "They would've needed a ladder to get up there, and if they did this in the middle of the night, I would have heard them. My bedroom window's right there." I stepped forward to look at it more closely.

The paint was too thick in places, cracked, and several chunks of it had fallen off to reveal the old wood underneath.

"Huh," I muttered to myself.

"See something?"

I reached out and scraped some of the paint into my hand. It flaked off easily, almost turning to dust instantly.

"This is the *old* paint," I said.

"But didn't you scrape everything before you started to – ?"

"I did. My hands were sore for a month." I looked up to the eaves, then followed the streak all the way back down. "I was particularly careful to get all the paint here on the porch – and I mean *all* of it. You know, so the front of the house'd look good when visitors showed up. Dad always used to say that you could get a little sloppy with the sides and back if you had to, but make damn sure the front looks good."

"Sounds like your dad. I sure miss seeing him and your mom around."

"That makes two of us."

"But at least they ain't suffering no more. They're in a better place."

"I know." Truth was, I *didn't* know – twelve years of Catholic school had left me a devout Agnostic, and many nights when I thought of my parents, I *wanted* to believe there was something more after this life, but I just . . . couldn't.

I sighed and slipped the paper under my arm. "Looks like I'm gonna have to trouble you for a ladder loan again."

"You know where it is. Come get it anytime. I can even whip up a pitcher of lemonade. The recipe's Ethel's, you know. Lord, that woman could whip up some tasty treats!"

"I remember the birthday cakes she used to make for me when I was a kid. She'd always cover it with foil, leave in front of the door, then ring the bell and hurry away before I saw it was her."

"That was my wife – Ethel Finney, the Birthday Cake Fairy."

"She never copped to it with me, you know."

He smiled. "She liked doing stuff like that." A wistful shadow crossed his face for a moment, then was gone. "Get whatever you need from my garage, then we'll have some lemonade."

"Thank you." Now it was my turn to shake my head. "I'm *positive* I scraped all the paint off before applying the new coats. And why would someone do something like this in the first place? As practical jokes go, it's kind of lame – not to mention rude."

"Takes all sorts to make a world, I guess."

We exchanged a few more pleasantries, shook hands again, and he started back to his garden. I was just opening the door when he called my name again and came up to the front steps.

"Don't tell me you saw another spot?" I said.

"No, no, it ain't that at all. Something just occurred to me. Back about fourteen, fifteen years ago when your dad was still alive, he wanted to paint this house 'cause he couldn't stand the way the white paint always showed every bit of dirt . . ."

" . . . yeah. . . ?"

"Well, I was out here one morning when he come out, and there was . . ." He stopped himself, then waved it away. "Never mind. You'd think I was getting senile."

"No, I wouldn't. I wish I had half as sharp a memory as yours." Which was true. Mom always used to say that Mr. Finney was the man to ask if there was something about the history of this neighborhood that you'd forgotten.

"Well," he said, "your dad come out here one morning and waved hello to me – I was workin' in the garden, big surprise – and he did the same thing you did, he got his paper and turned around, and there was a streak of paint –" He pointed to the front porch. "– right in that same spot. Eaves to porch, just like this one. He cussed up a storm and we went to take a look and found out the paint was still wet." He stood staring for a moment – not at me or the house or the streak, but into the depths of a past that was probably more alive to him than the world he was stuck in now – and suddenly blanched.

Thinking he might be having a heart attack or something, I went down and put a hand on his arm. "You okay?"

"Yeah, yeah," he said, snapping from his reverie. "It's just that . . . I remember your dad cussing about the damn kids that'd done it, painting a streak of 'workman's grey' down the front of the house." He gave a short laugh. "This is gonna sound nuts, but I'd almost swear to you that that streak of paint your dad found was the exact same color the house is now."

"I don't remember him asking me to help him clean it," I said.

"That's just it," said Mr. Finney. "He didn't have to clean it. We found it around eight-thirty in the morning, and it was gone when we looked again around ten."

"Gone?"

"Uh-huh." He looked at his watch, then at me. "Guess you think I'm weird, huh?"

I knew what he was getting at. "We'll see at ten," I replied. "Meet you by the curb?"

"I'll be there."

I always used to wonder where, precisely, the soul is located. If the soul is to be found in space, then where the hell is it? Physicists think of time and space as a sort of four-dimensional sheet with the possibilities of other disconnected sheets. Could the soul reside in between the layers? On the other hand, spacetime could be envisioned as enfolded by, or embedded in, a higher dimensional space, much as a two-dimensional surface or sheet is embedded in three-dimensional space. So why couldn't the soul inhabit a location in this higher dimensional space which is still, geometrically speaking, close to our own physical space-time, but not actually in *it?*

If that's the case, then could it be that that "smallest, unseen" quantity – the 1.62 x 10^{33} *at which space and time come apart – is actually the location where the soul physically goes to roost after death?*

3. One Foot in History/The Weight

Back in the house, I laughed to myself. There were a hundred explanations for what had happened – both with Dad and with me – but if Mr. Finney was trying to turn his morning into a short romp through *The Twilight Zone,* who was I to ruin his fun?

I poured myself another cup of coffee and went to the refrigerator for an orange.

I opened the door and discovered the bags of Ayds setting on the top shelf.

I was still staring at them when my sister, Blair, came up behind me, pointed at the bags, and said, "Mommy."

"Huh?"

She looked at me as if I were some sort of dim-witted puppy. *"Mommy's candy."*

"Oh. Thanks for clearing that –"

Then it hit me. When I was teenager and Blair was barely two (she was a late-in-life baby), our mother went through a phase where, for some reason, she decided she needed to lose weight. Despite her weighing probably one hundred twenty pounds soaking wet, she started buying and gobbling Ayds by the bagful, so no matter what, there were always several bags of it – say three pounds' worth – in our fridge, same shelf, same spot.

I stared at the bags and whispered, " . . . jesus. . . ."

I inherited our parents' house (along with the care

of my sister) after Mom's death. I've replaced most of the appliances in the kitchen, except for the refrigerator. It's the same one my parents bought right after they were married, and soon will celebrate its fiftieth year of operation. The damn thing's a wonder; it has never, *ever* broken down.

I pulled out one of the bags just to look at it. I was holding something that, to the best of my knowledge, had not existed since I was fifteen. Blair stomped her foot and put her hands on her hips, her lower lip jutting out in a pout that would look right at home on a three-year-old's face. "Thas' Mommy's candy," she said. "Gonna get it if you eat any."

Blair has Down's Syndrome. She's creeping up on thirty but has the mental capacity and verbal skills of a six-year-old. The doctors were certain she wouldn't live through her teen years, but she's beaten the odds. Hell, she'll probably live to bury me. She lives with me because I promised Mom and Dad that I would not put her into any sort of home . . . and because of a certain piece of advice Mom gave me at the end of her life.

I don't keep Blair closed off from the rest of the world; she attends a sheltered workshop five days a week where they teach her basic social and personal skills – what they refer to as "habilitation training" – and she has many friends. Hers is as fine a life as I can provide for her on what little is left from my parents' insurance (after final medical bills and burial expenses) and what I make as day manager and co-owner of Cedar Hill's largest and most successful used bookstore. Believe me when I tell you that "successful" is a bit of a euphemism when applied here, but the store's got a sufficiently large enough clientele and a good enough reputation that business is steady. Steady enough. Thank God the house is paid for.

Blair came over and yanked the bag from my hand, tearing it open and scattering dozens of wrapped pieces all over the kitchen floor. She stepped back, dropped the mangled remains of the bag, and gasped. "Oh . . . lookee what you made me do."

"*I* didn't make you do anything," I snapped, with a bit too much irritation under the surface. "You did this all by yourself. If you wanted to see it, I would have given it to you, but you didn't ask. *Did you?*"

She glared at me, hands fisting at her sides. She chewed on her lower lip, took a deep breath, and then spit on the floor. *"Pancakes!"*

Caring for Blair takes up nearly all of my non-work and -sleeping time. Most days she's well-behaved, but she has these episodes, usually lasting two or three days at a time once they start, where she hates the world as well as everyone and everything in it. I've often wondered if these "spells" (as Dad used to call them) are triggered by some complex realization somewhere in her mind that she's different from a lot of people, and this realization makes her angry and hateful. And *hateful* is definitely the word for it.

I pointed to the candy and the spit. "I'm not cleaning that up."

"Don't care."

"I think you should apologize for what you said."

"No."

"Blair. . . ." The warning in my voice was clear.

She glowered at me for a few seconds longer, then stomped over to the kitchen counter, picked up the sugar canister, and dumped its contents on top of the spit and candy. Then she slammed the canister down so hard it bounced a foot into the air and came back down with half its circumference smashed in.

"Stop it," I said.

Her response was to spit again – this time at me.

Like I said: hateful.

She was hating me, hating that it was Saturday and there was no workshop to attend, hating that I never let her go anywhere alone, not even to the little market at the end of the street, and most of all hating that I would make her clean up this mess. So she spit on the floor and growled her version of "Fuck you!" at me. (Blair has her own special meanings for several words: "Pancakes" is *Fuck You*; "MamaFrog" – one word, two caps – is *My Period Has Started*; "Skateboard" is *Time To Watch Television*; and "Kahoutek" – one she learned from me during my brief but infamous Astronomy Craze of 1974 – is what she says instead of *Gesundheit.* That one gets weird looks and big laughs from people every time.)

I grabbed the broom from its place beside the pantry and held it out. Blair stomped her feet and released one of her patented tantrum screams, then wrenched the broom from my hand and did a Babe Ruth with it right upside my head, snapping the handle in half, bloodying my nose, and leaving most of the bristles stuck in my hair, beard, and face.

I reached up and wiped away some of the blood, then sat on the floor looking up at her. Blair has a very powerful swing, and an even worse right cross. I've been on the receiving end of both more times than I care to remember.

"Do you feel better now?"

"Pancakes! *Pancakes! PANCAKES!*"

I shook my head and continued to sit there, too tired to get mad about it. In a little while she'd start feeling really awful about what she'd done, come to me all hugs and apologies, and things would go on as they had before until she had another "spell" later tonight, or tomorrow. This was always the pattern. For the next seventy-two hours, life was going to be a miserable proposition.

There followed several moments of silence. Blair would either blow up again, or go to her room to listen to records or the radio, or scribble on one of her dozens of sketch pads (Blair loves to draw and water-paint).

I waited, hoping it would go no further than this – which thus far had been mild in comparison to some of her fits. She once broke my nose when I forgot to pick up microwave popcorn for our Friday Night Movie. (Blair has broken my nose twice.) Another time she came out of the bathroom and threw a *very* used, very bloody tampon right in my face. I never did find out what that had been about.

One of the things I hate about myself is those times – usually post-fit – when I think about how much easier my life would be if, A) Blair were living in a group home, or, B) If she'd never been born.

I know – that second one is unforgivable. But it's there, and eventually I'd have to deal with it. Just not now, not *then,* not that morning.

I reached up and pulled the paper towel roll from the counter and used about a thousand sheets to wipe away the blood from my nose and hands – some of the bristles had managed to scrape my fingers enough to draw blood.

I finished, then sat back against the wall and – my nostrils stuffed full of torn paper towel – leaned back my head, and swallowed.

I was surprised to feel tears in my eyes. I quickly wiped them away before they spilled down my face. Christ, what was the point sometimes? I'd had such *dreams* in this house and in this kitchen when I was growing up: I was going to be an astronaut (a ruptured spleen at age six killed that one), then I was going to be a rock 'n' roll star (had to hock my guitars and amplifier when I was fifteen to help out with money when Dad was laid off from the plant for a while), and then, in college, I was going to be either a great writer or a great scientist (I minored in English and Physics and never got around to doing a damn thing with either degree).

I used to laugh at the part of myself that thought black light posters were cool and that I was going to take on the world and win, but at times like this I realized that something of that teenaged soul lived on and watched me, like a child ashamed of its parents. Only now I was my own parent and my own child. No part gets left by the side of the road; each ghost of yourself at ten, or thirteen, or sixteen, sits in judgment of what the others did, and what they have become.

I pulled in a deep breath that hurt more than I'd expected.

"Don't cry, Danny," said Blair.

"I'm not," I lied.

"Yes, you are." Her voice was thin and scared. She'd only seen me cry twice before this; once at Dad's funeral, once at Mom's. Blair equated my tears with death. In a way, I guess she was right to make that connection this time.

"Danny?" She sounded on the verge of tears herself. I waved my hand at her, a sign for her to be quiet and leave me alone for a minute.

Sometimes, when the past sneaks up behind you, it's hard to shake it off right away.

My "coming of age" happened between 1971 and 1976. I was too young to "relate" (yeech – *that word!)* to the World War II generation and not old enough to be accepted by the Woodstock Nation; D-Day happened long before I took my first breath, and by the time I understood that the Kent State shootings were related to some war in a place called Vietnam, President Nixon was beginning the process of pulling U.S. troops out of the sad and ravaged country while thousands of ragged Cambodian refugees traversed the endless Killing Fields in hopes of being air-lifted by the U.N. to a safer land. So there I was, like others my age, dismissed by the ones who'd fought the Nazi Terror and mocked by those who wore flowers in their hair and made the "peace" sign and quoted people with names like Leary and Hoffman and Dylan and Biaz. Abandoned to our own devices, m-m-m-my g-generation inherited a Teenage Wasteland and grew up in front of the television set with Flip Wilson and the Bradys and Fred Sanford and the eminently-quotable Archie Bunker while looking for our niche. I spent a lot of time listening to Yes and King Crimson and Emerson, Lake & Palmer and other denizens of the short-lived "art rock" era: From the Beginning they sang of being Close to the Edge, of seeing All Good People going Roundabout in the Court of the Crimson King. Mysticism abounded in their lyrics, and even though it wasn't easy to fully understand their sometimes nebulous concepts, their music nonetheless planted a notion in my mind that maybe, just maybe, we of the Brushed Aside Age could strive toward some new level of universal understanding (aided by the smoke of Hawaiian Seedless, natch) and salvage Purpose from the labyrinthine chaos left by one Depression, four wars, an energy crisis, and the "Generation Gap." Yeah, we were full of shit, I know that now – but then, *then* it felt good to believe in that, to be a young armchair anarchist who could lay waste to the establishment during the day and still get home in time for supper and *Night Gallery*; it felt good to be full of piss and vinegar and passion, knowing there was a reason for being alive, there was such Promise for us to fulfill . . . then four buffoons broke into a suite at the Watergate Hotel and before you could say "Woodward and Bernstein" our unbeknownst-to-us fragile idealism crumpled into a heap on the floor. By the time we were able to stand again it was 1977; a new movie that no one knew much about called *Star Wars* had just opened, Menachem Begin was the leader of Israel, four other buffoons tried to steal Elvis Presley's body, and *Studio 54* opened its doors. We took our cue from this latter event: dressed in polyester leisure suits with open collars and gold chains dangling around our neck, possessed by a Saturday Night Fever that jackhammered under mirror-ball lights, we boogied across the disco floor in revealing dresses, flared pants, fuck-me pumps, and platform shoes. We were the selfish, hedonistic "Me" generation, sexually liberated and not giving a rat's ass about anything that did not directly affect us. Our so-called values were the supreme embarrassment of the last half-century – c'mon, already, we thought *Jonathan Livingston Seagull* was deep and were *proud* of ourselves for inventing the Pet Rock, the Mood Ring, and Space Food Sticks. We were blissfully ignorant of any ugliness in the world . . . then the Rev. Jim Jones led his followers to mass-suicide in Guyana, Mark David Chapman walked up to John Lennon outside the Dakota Hotel in New York and splattered the former Beatles' brains all over the pavement, someone decided to check John Wayne Gacy's basement after he was arrested, and those of us still left standing realized that no amount of self-indulgence or blind loyalty to false ideals was going to protect us from the Big Dark Eventuality; so the leisure suits and plats and pumps were stored far away in the backs of closets where no one would ever have to look upon them again, a thing called AIDS (definitely *not* spelled with a "y") came to collect for our careless promiscuity, and we stood before the looking glass of our conscience wondering why we felt so empty. How romantic to be so disillusioned at such an early age.

Some of us never got over it. Some of us didn't even survive it. The rest of us . . . well, we managed to get out alive and grew up to become uncomfortable anachronisms. And co-owners of used bookstores.

My little stroll down Amnesia Lane over, I looked up at my sister and said, "Why don't you go watch some cartoons? I'll be along in a few minutes."

"I didn't mean to hurt you."

"But you did."

She looked like she was going to break down any second.

"I'm sorry I said that, Blair. I know you didn't mean to. It's okay."

"Really?"

"Yes."

"I love you lots, Danny."

"I love you too." And I did. But at times like this, I wished I didn't. So sue me.

Blair exhaled and folded her arms across her chest, the unsteadiness gone from her voice. Now it was her turn to sound like an adult and make *me* feel better. "I made a mess."

"I noticed."

"An' I hit you."

"Uh-huh."

"An' I busted the broom."

"You'll get my bill in the mail."

She laughed. When I looked at her she quickly covered her mouth with her hands so I wouldn't see the grin.

"What's so funny?"

"You. You're goofy!"

"No, I am not goofy. I am bleeding. Do you think that's funny?"

"Yes."

"Well, it isn't," I said, rising to my feet. As I was doing so, I caught a glimpse of my reflection in the big silver toaster: My hair was a mess, my shirt was speckled with paint dust and drops of blood, and the pieces of paper towel I'd stuffed into my nose – pieces which I thought had been about the size of a fingernail – looked like the tusks on a sick walrus.

I couldn't help it – I laughed too. Then Blair laughed louder. Then I really let fly, guffawing so hard that I blew one of the walrus tusks out of my nose.

"All right," I said. "I guess this makes me goofy."

Blair found the dustpan and grabbed my still-folded newspaper. "I clean up my mess now." She knelt down and started to use the paper for a sweeping device.

"I haven't read that yet," I said, taking it from her.

"But I gotta –"

"I know, I know." I looked around and spotted the remains of a pizza box in the recycling bin. I tore off the lid, folded it in half, and handed it to her. "Use this."

"Wow," she said. "That was a smart thing."

"Well, even us goofy bleeding guys have our moments." That got another laugh from her.

Triumphant in my duty to entertain, I took a small bow and headed into the downstairs bathroom.

Then there's the question of time itself. If the soul is not in space, then is it in time? Does it exist somewhere in that moment where 1.62 x 10^{33} *separates time and space? If the soul is the true source of our perceptions, then that has to include our perception of time. How else do you explain that so many of our mental processes are time-dependent: planning, hoping, regretting, mourning, anticipating, cha-cha-cha?*

The idea of a timeless soul has always troubled me. What

meaning do we attach to the soul after death, if the before-after relationship that we call time is transcended by souls?

Physicists do not regard time as a sequence of events which simply happen. Instead, all of the past and future are simply there, *and time extends in either direction from any given moment in much the same way space stretches away from any given particular place. So the there that the physicists refer to, we call the present: a simple point on the four-dimensional sheet of the universe – a dot in the middle of a page.*

But the ghost of a dot or a word or a drawing erased from a page can be brought back again.

Palimpsest.

4. Time Was/Hello It's Me

I cleaned my cuts, applied Band-Aids, and used small squares of toilet paper until my nose stopped bleeding.

While I was waiting for my nose to get its act together, I sat on the lid of the toilet and opened the paper.

At first I thought the paper might have landed in a small puddle of some kind and the ink was starting to bleed through the pages, but it didn't feel damp at all; it looked, felt, and smelled like a fresh-off-the-press newspaper.

Each page looked to have been printed on twice: two pages superimposed on top of each other. The print and photos of one layer were dark enough to be read and seen if you could ignore the lighter but nonetheless quite visible ghost page underneath. This wouldn't be the first time that the *Cedar Hill Ally* experienced trouble with its print run, nor would it be the last. This is a town that likes to think of itself as a city, and despite everything the city government says it wants to do, Big Changes aren't really in their plans, they just like to make a lot of noise so those of us still living here will feel that Cedar Hill matters in the larger scheme of things. So they talk about updating the printing facilities at the *Ally* with computerized, state-of-the-art equipment, but it remains, as always, a small-town paper with small-town paper printing equipment.

I was ready to stuff the whole thing into the recycling bin when something on page two (or I should say ghost-page twelve) caught my attention.

The 1975 Senior Class of Cedar Hill High School would conduct graduation ceremonies this Thursday at White's Field, starting at one p.m.

Not a reunion. Graduation.

My graduating class, in fact.

I angled the paper away from the light to cut down on the glare, flipping through the other pages to make out what I could of the ghost pages beneath.

Every local, national, and international story was dated June 21, 1975.

I turned to the Community Announcements page.

William and Ethel Finney of 190 North Tenth Street would be celebrating their fortieth wedding anniversary on the 28th.

Then I looked at The Now Playing page.

The Midland Theater was showing *Tommy.* The Auditorium was featuring *The Other Side of the Mountain.* Cinema 4 (then a real phenomenon, one building with *four different movie theaters! Can you imagine that?)* was showing *Dog Day Afternoon, French Connection 2, Hearts of the West,* and *The Apple Dumpling Gang.*

Finally, the Birth Announcements.

The previous day, Mrs. Virginia Gabriel of 182 North Tenth Street had given birth to a daughter, Blair Ann, at six-fifteen p.m. A parenthetical aside noted that, although there had been some "unexpected complications," mother and daughter were doing well and expected to be released sometime in the next forty-eight hours.

Unexpected Complications. Right.

Mom had been fifty-one when she'd given birth to Blair, Dad had just turned fifty-five. They each lived only twelve more years, dying within six months of each other. Neither of them had any idea how to deal with a Down's Syndrome baby.

I thought about what Mom had said to me during that last visit:

"I knew we were taking an awful chance. I mean, I hadn't gone through the Change yet – which had me worried something terrible – and now here I was about to have another baby. I heard all these terrible stories about woman my age who'd had babies come out in the most *terrible* state . . . and it scared me, Daniel, right down to the ground.

"I never told your dad about this, and I don't know why I'm telling you now, but before I do, you've got to promise me that you'll never, *ever* let on to Blair. You promise? Swear to me, Daniel. Okay, then.

"I knew going into my second month that something was wrong with the baby inside me. Don't ask me *how* I knew, I just . . . I just *did*, that's all. A woman's body, it speaks a language to her heart that only she can understand, and my body was telling me that what was inside me wasn't right somehow. Don't look at me like that, it wasn't like some *Rosemary's Baby* or *Omen* thing, I never once thought I was carrying Satan's bastard son – well, maybe once, but then you came out and looked so sweet . . . that was a joke, stop looking at me that way.

"I didn't think that Blair was a monster or anything, I just knew that she wasn't going to be *right.* I didn't think me and your dad could handle it, not at our ages and him with all his nerve problems – who knew his heart was going on him then? So I started thinking about . . . likelihoods."

Likelihoods. That was the word she used. In the early half of the 1970s, in a middle-class neighborhood (technically *lower* middle-class) in a sad little Midwestern town like Cedar Hill, a pregnant fifty-one-year-old woman with a husband and son, a pregnant fifty-one-year-old woman who helped organize community charity drives and bake sales and played Bridge with her friends every Thursday night, who never talked back to her husband and was raised to believe that a woman's place was in the home and only in the home, this type of woman, for whom appearances and others' opinions of her mattered greatly, this type of woman never said, whispered, or even *thought* the word 'abortion.'

But that didn't mean she wouldn't come up with a word such as *likelihoods* and assign it the same definition.

"I wasn't sure how I was going to do it. I never thought about it being like they scream now-days – you know, a sin, murder, all of that – I just knew that if me and your dad had this baby, our lives would be changed for the worse. Your dad was trying to figure out if he could retire early, and I knew that if we had this baby, he'd be working right up until the day he died . . . and that's just what happened.

"Don't think bad of me, hon, okay? I love Blair, I do . . . but even now I can say that I never really wanted her. I couldn't figure out if I should go to a doctor or a priest or maybe go ask one of the girls who were forming those Women's Lib clubs at O.S.U. I had no idea how a woman my age back then went about getting that kind of information. You heard all them horror stories about girls who went down to Mexico and got themselves all butchered up and died . . . just terrible.

"So I finally thought to myself, 'If I'm supposed to have this baby, then have it I will . . . but if I'm *not* supposed to, then let Fate provide the means.'

"Turned out that Fate was listening to me that day.

"You remember how there used to be that piece of carpeting at the top of the stairs that everybody used to trip on? Lord, it was a miracle you or your father never fell and broke your necks!

"Anyway, one night I couldn't sleep, so I got up and went out into the hall and just . . . just stood there, wondering what I was going to do. I decided to go down to the kitchen and make a glass of warm Ovaltine, and just as I got to the landing, my foot got caught in that piece of carpet and I almost fell. If it hadn't been for me grabbing the railing, I think I would've – and you know what a tumble that would have been.

"Then I just sat there on the top step and cried for a minute, because I realized that I'd just thrown away the chance Fate had given me. So I went down and made my Ovaltine, and while I sat there drinking it, I got to thinking . . . maybe I could do it again – you know, get my foot caught and fall. It wasn't enough of a fall to kill you, but if you were pregnant, it would be enough to make you lose a baby. I know because . . . I never told you this before, but . . . you weren't our first child. I was pregnant before you, and one day about a month or so into my pregnancy, I was carrying a small basket of laundry downstairs and slipped at the top of the stairs and fell. I miscarried right on the spot.

"So why couldn't I do it again? I mean, all I suffered that first time was a broken wrist and some cuts and bruises. I decided to do it.

"I went back up and stood there, making sure the carpet was still gonna catch my foot, and then I did a couple of rehearsal trips, you know? Taking a few steps back and then going forward, not looking down to see where I was going. Caught my foot each time.

"I got ready to do it for real, I walked a good ways back down the hall to make sure I had some speed behind me, and just when I got to the edge and felt my foot slip under, I felt this . . . this *breeze* behind me, like something big was flying by, or somebody tried reaching out for me. At the same time, I saw this little light from the corner of my eye, and I thought, 'I just felt the wings of an angel trying to grab me.' I had just enough time to stick out my arms and stop myself from falling – and I would've. I'd been given the *real* sign I asked for. So I went back to bed and said no more about it, and that's how you came to have Blair for a sister."

Blair knocked on the bathroom door. "You okay, Danny?"

It was only then I realized I'd been in there for almost half and hour. "Uh, yeah, yeah. I'm okay."

"I cleaned up."

"That's good. Thank you."

Silence for a moment, then: "I got something for you." A hint of mischief in her voice. Her mood was back to normal now. I still wondered when the next fit would come.

I folded up the paper and opened the bathroom door. "What is it?"

"I got you a girlfriend."

I blinked. "Huh?"

Blair nodded. "I found her on the back porch."

She grabbed my hand and dragged me back into the kitchen.

Sitting at the table, a large, heavy-looking back-pack resting by one of her legs, her long black hair as thick and beautiful as I'd remembered it, was Laura Kirwan, the woman who I once thought was the love of my life.

"Hey, stranger," she said, a hint of Is-He-Glad-To-See-Me-Or-Not? in her voice. "Blair let me in."

"Why the back door?"

She shook her head and laughed, the same deep-throated laugh that had only gotten sexier with age. "Dumbass. Don't you remember? Everyone used to come in through the back door when we were in high school."

"Oh." I am nothing if not a flaming wit.

She looked at Blair, then at me. "It's good to see you."

"You too."

"I wasn't so sure you'd want to see me. I mean, what with the way I left."

I shrugged. "I'm sure you had your reasons."

I knew that at a moment like this I should be pulling her to her feet and holding her close, hugging her for all I was worth – God, she still made my heart triple its rhythm – but I couldn't. I suddenly felt like a failure. How many evenings had she and I spent talking over our dreams and hopes? Here we were, twenty-five years later, like two characters from a Harry Chapin song, knowing what we felt but having no idea what to do about it. . . .

Palimpsest.

When copying Biblical texts, ancient monks were often forced to erase pictures and words from previously-used sheets of parchment because they lacked sufficient supplies of paper. As the ink from these newly-created pages began to dry, the impressions left on the parchment from what had been there before began to show through. View these pages in their modern-day museum homes and it's easy to see where the original drawings and text "ghost" through, creating two simultaneous pages on one sheet; past and present merged into one: the former bleeding into the latter, as if living already for the second time.

But is this life, like that of the soul, in time or space?

5. *I've Been to Paradise (But I've Never Been to Me)/Now I'm Here*

It was 1975 the first and only time I told Laura Kirwan that I loved her.

Ours was one of those oddball relationships that you see manifest in high school. I was the nerd, she was the popular cheerleader/student council/homecoming queen/straight-A student who everyone wanted to know. Hell, guys like me could simply revel in her breeze as she passed us in the hall. That was enough; just to know that someone like her existed in our world and we got to see her.

I was never really sure of why she started talking to me before the study hall we had together, I knew only that I felt humbled that she did.

At first it was simply about school and teenager stuff – which teachers we liked, which ones we thought were dweebs, what movies we thought looked good – but then things started getting a bit more serious.

The first time she'd had sex with Paul Lawrence, a star player on the football team and her boyfriend our junior year, it wasn't exactly consensual. In fact, as she told me about it, we both realized at the same time that it had been rape (the term "date-rape" wouldn't be around for another twenty years, but, still it was rape), pure and simple. However, Paul was very popular, as was she, and the Popular People simply didn't cause any fuss. I told her she should have him arrested and charged, but she was both too humiliated and too scared of how it would affect her social standing in the school to do anything about.

"I'll just break up with him and warn the other girls away," she said.

"Yeah, that'll teach him." I made no attempt to disguise my disapproval.

She glared at me. "I thought you were my friend."

"I am."

"Then would you please not judge me about this? Just . . . just be my friend, okay? Just understand."

"I'll try."

We sat together in study hall every day after that, and had lunch together at least twice a week. Being around her leant me a certain mystique among her circle of friends: If *Laura Kirwan* likes this guy, then maybe he's got something we haven't noticed before.

Hey, it got me a couple of dates with girls who otherwise wouldn't have given me a first look, let alone a second one. But that didn't matter; by our senior year, I was so in love with Laura that I couldn't imagine the rest of my life being worth squat without her.

After-School Specials have won Emmys with less material to work from.

But she cast me in the role of best friend/surrogate brother, and I hated it, but I'd never tell her that because it would mean an end to our time together.

Like our "study nights" that were really just an excuse to watch movies, listen to records, gossip about the people we knew, and share our hopes for the future with someone who wasn't going to laugh at our dreams.

Then came the Friday night when she didn't bring any books or records or magazines over. She came to the back door and knocked – even though she knew it was okay to just come in – and I answered to find her standing there in tears, carrying her favorite backpack, the one I'd gotten her for her birthday last year.

"Laura? What's wrong? Get in here."

It was a little before eleven p.m. I had the house to myself for the weekend, Mom and Dad having gone to visit friends in Indiana for Mom's birthday. I pulled Laura into the house and she dragged me into the darkened living room where she stood shuddering and weeping.

"What's going on?"

"I brought you some flowers. Here."

I took them from her without looking at them. "What is it?"

"I just needed to see you, that's all. To let you know something."

I had been listening to an album on the stereo and trying to take a nap; the volume of the music was as low as the lights. I moved to turn the lights on and the music off but before I could, Laura grabbed me and kissed me and pulled me down to the floor.

It took a few moments for the full impact of what was happening to register – how many times had I fantasized about this exact thing? – but when it did register, I decided not to question it.

I fumbled around her body for the better part of an hour, daring to touch one of her breasts, then another, then haphazardly sliding my hand under her blouse to unhook her bra. I broke away from her kisses only long enough to gulp down air and occasionally wipe the sweat off my face and the saliva (hers, mine, *ours)* from my chin.

She pulled away from me, one hand on my chest, the other squeezing the back of my neck, and looked at me with her pale green eyes as if she were a kindergarten teacher facing a sad, slow-witted child. "Do you like the flowers?"

"Yeah," I said, not knowing if I meant it or not. She'd brought me a bunch of huge red flowers that she said had to immediately be put in water because they were red hibiscuses and they only lived for a day.

No girl had ever given me flowers before.

"I wanted you to have them so you'll remember how . . . special this evening has to be. There'll probably be better times than this, maybe even a *best* time, but there's only one first time. Do you understand?"

The delicate vulnerability in her eyes – eyes with sad, dark places around them that gave the impression when she laughed that she was hiding an oft-broken heart behind a scrim of gaiety – was enough to kill you.

Mustering all my self-control, I touched her face and said, "More than you know."

She stood and began to disrobe in a slow, promising way. "Don't touch your clothes," she said. "I want to undress you."

Her fingers went to work on my shirt and belt, my socks and shoes, my pants and underwear as if they were playing a glissando over piano keys. The ninety or so seconds it took for her to strip me naked me were agony; exquisite agony.

Then we lay down on the floor and made unhurried, quiet, intensely satisfying love, careful not to make even the slightest sound; the secrecy of the sex, the underlying Is-this-where-that-goes-and-are-you-sure-it-doesn't-hurt panic – all of it had added to the urgency and made the sex even steamier. Throughout all of it she chewed on piece of strawberry flavored bubblegum like it was sweet sacred mouthful of forbidden dirty. (To this day I can't see a teenaged girl chew gum without getting a raging hard-on.) For a few astonishing moments, as Greg Lake's richly resonant voice rolled from the speakers and sang of love that would flood darkness with light, we melted into the natural rhythms of our bodies, a rhythm that was ours and ours alone, Danny and Laura, my body and hers, in the clearest physical connection one body can make to another; I sank inside of her, her breath the humid warmth of sunlight against my bare shoulder as her pelvis thrust and her nipples hardened and her hands clamped together at the base of my spine and Lake sang and she sighed, then softly groaned and I swallowed a scream and we felt ourselves shudder as we spread out warmly from the center of our bodies to become something grander than we'd been before, a thing unseen in a place unknown where we were no longer alone behind our flesh.

Afterward we lay facing each other, fingertips touching, bodies lacquered in sweat, voices barely more than spirit-whispers among the shadows, and spoke of the secret things that two people who have just savored the moist, vulnerable intimacy of each other's bodies feel compelled to reveal.

I told her I wanted to freeze the world in this moment forever; that way, her flowers would never die and we could stay just as we were. She smiled, brushed my lips with hers, then draped one of her legs over my hip and held my face in her hands.

"I could swallow you whole," she said.

"I might like that." I eased her onto her back and began kissing her everywhere, endlessly, and just as I was parting her legs, tongue at the ready, she gently gripped a handful of my hair and stopped me.

"Don't want too much," she said.

"I can't get enough of you."

She traced along my jaw with her index finger. "Be careful. With some people, even a little bit is too much."

"You sound so serious."

"And you look so wrecked. The sweat on your face looks like tears. That's why I said that. Don't ever cry for me, okay? Promise me that, that you won't ever cry for me?"

Even then it seemed she knew her life would take a downward spiral, but that thought flashed across my mind only briefly; I was too horny to think about anything other than the moist, inviting treat only inches from my mouth.

"I promise." I started in on her, but she jerked back and sat up, pulling her knees up against her chest.

"Listen to me, okay? I know this's going to sound weird, but . . . okay, you *lose* things along the way, right? I don't mean stuff, I mean other things, things" – she touched the part of her chest where her heart was –"in here. And you can feel the empty spaces sometimes and it hurts." She looked at me. "You have no idea what I'm talking about, do you?"

"No."

"You know what I want? I want to live in a song. Does that sound stupid? I know most people want their lives to be like a movie or book but I want . . . I want

'Drift Away' and 'The First Time Ever I Saw Your Face' and 'Join Together'. I want tenderness and romance and poetic proclamations of love, I want to dance in the rain at midnight in Paris. I want to be like the music I love. To be Maggie May and Layla and Julie-Julie-Julie Do You Love Me. But I know that's never going to happen. I wish you *could* freeze the world right now. The flowers would never die and I'd never grow any older than I am right now, I'd never have to worry about watching everything . . . fade."

I tried to take her hands but she wouldn't let me touch her. "What's wrong?"

She wiped her eyes, then stood up and began putting on her clothes. "Was I all right? Did you like it?"

She sounded so mournful, so lonely and scared, that all I could say was, "I love you, Laura. I always will."

She kissed me, long and tenderly, then pulled something out of her book-bag: a Polaroid camera, the instant kind. She turned on one of the table lamps and I saw how happy, how joyous she looked.

At that moment, I knew that I would never see anything so beautiful as she was *right now.*

"You're the first guy who's ever said he loves me." She handed me the camera, stood back, and began straightening her hair with her fingers, then stopped. "No. I want to capture this just as I am right now. Will you take my picture so I'll always know what I looked like the first time someone said they loved me?"

"We'll put it in a photo album," I said. "We can even write a caption beneath: 'The First Time Ever I Saw Your Face.'"

Her smile was starlight. "You really meant it, didn't you?"

"Yes," I said, getting her in frame. "I love you."

Starlight, starbright; Laura-there, Laura-now.

The camera flashed, grumbled, and whirred. The

photo came sliding out.

She snatched it away and held it against her chest, then quickly plucked one of the red hibiscuses from its stem and wrapped it in a fresh Kleenex.

"What're you doing?" I said. "I want to –"

"No," she said, laughing almost giddily. She reached into her bag and took out a thin hardback book, *The Poems of Christina Rossetti,* flipped to a specific page, then carefully placed the flower and undeveloped photo inside and snapped it closed.

"But I –"

"Shh," she said. God, she was so radiant. "No, you can't see it, and neither can I. Don't you understand what you've given to me, Danny? Do you have any idea what you've done?"

" . . . uh, *no* . . ."

"You've frozen the world for me, and I'll always love you for it. From now on, regardless of what happens, I'll always have *this time,* preserved just the way it was – the way it is right now. And someday, when I really need to feel good again, when I need to have something to look forward to, when I need to be reminded that there was a time when everything was perfect and I was loved, I will open this book, and I will take out the flower and the picture, and I will see for the first time what I looked like on the night you told me that you loved me, and maybe that will be enough to make everything new again so I can go on."

She knew; even then, she knew.

We finished dressing, then went into the kitchen. I was going to fix us something to eat when the headlights from a car shone in the window from the driveway.

"I have to go now, Danny."

"What? Why? What's going on?" I reached out to take her hand and she pulled away.

"I c-can't, Danny. I . . ." She looked like someone who suddenly had the weight of the world dumped on their shoulders and didn't dare tell anyone for fear it might crush her.

"Laura, *what is it?*"

She didn't say anything, only stepped forward, put her arms around my neck, and gave me the longest, sweetest, saddest kiss I'd ever had or ever would receive.

Then she put her head on my shoulder and stood there holding me.

"Did Tanner do something?" I asked. It was the first time I dared speak his name since she arrived. Tim Tanner was her latest boyfriend, another football player who also played basketball.

"I have to go away for a while, Danny."

Listen to how my chest cracked open at those words.

"Tell me what's wrong!"

"I can't. I just wanted to stop by and tell you . . . that I. . . ." She shook her head and touched my face.

"Please don't go, Laura," I said, ashamed of the scared-little-boy tone in my voice. "I don't want you to leave. You're my . . . I mean . . . ah, hell! I love you, Laura. I think I've loved you since the moment I first saw you."

"There's my Danny, sweet, romantic, never judging me."

"Don't. Go. *Please.*" I was crying now and hating myself for showing her just how weak I could be when she needed someone to be strong.

"Promise me one thing."

"What?"

"Don't cry for me, okay? Just remember that you were the only guy who . . . who I believed when he told me that he loved me."

She grabbed her bag and ran off the porch, disappearing around the front of the house. I ran through the kitchen and living room, through the front door, and vaulted down the front steps just in time to see her pull away in Tanner's car.

Now, twenty-five years later, sitting in my kitchen, she smiled at me and said, "Did you keep your promise, Danny?"

"What're you – ?"

"You never cried for me, did you?"

"He was crying today," said Blair.

Laura looked at her, then me. "Is anything wrong?"

"No, a bad morning, that's all."

"Well, what do we do now?"

"Why are you here, Laura?"

Her answer came immediately, with the sure, steady cadence of someone who had practiced what they were going to say so they'd get it right: "You may find this hard to believe, Danny, but there hasn't been a day since I left Cedar Hill when I haven't thought about you and what we could've had if I hadn't been so stupid and full of myself. I was *popular,* after all, and you weren't, and I didn't want to risk my place in the school's hierarchy by getting romantically involved with you.

"I knew the night I left that I'd made the first truly big mistake of my life by not staying with you. But by then I was pregnant with Tanner's kid and the two of us were going to run off with his college money and start a life for ourselves. I couldn't tell you – I couldn't tell anyone. I lost the baby, he got bored with me, and less than seven months after we left this burg, he dumped me in L.A. with two hundred dollars and one suitcase of clothes."

"How'd you manage to get by?"

She smiled but there was no humor in it. "I was a pretty young thing. It wasn't hard to find work – no, I didn't start hooking or anything like that." She shrugged. "Made some movies – not the kind they would've shown at the Midland, but it paid the bills. I got involved with a guy who knew what to do with money, how to invest it, and between that and the movies, I got by just fine. You're making me stray off the point – I always loved you, Danny. I still do – and I think you must still feel something for me or else you'd've kicked my ass out the door thirty seconds after you saw me."

"Instant repeat of a question I asked a quarter-century ago: What's going on, Laura?"

She stared at her hands. "If you're asking me if there's been some big dramatic turn of events, then the answer is 'nothing.' Three days ago I was sitting in my apartment in L.A. watching television, and *French Connection 2* was on. I remembered how you always used to rave how it was every bit as good as the original –"

"– better, in some ways – hell, John Frankenheimer had some sequences –"

"– could we not do our Roger Ebert imitations right now? So I watched it, and you were right, it's great, Hackman's even better in it than he was in the first one, and all of a sudden I wanted to talk to you about it, about why Frankenheimer's your favorite movie director, about why you still own LPs when most everything is available on CD, about anything and everything, the way we used to in high school. And then I realized that what I wanted was . . . you.

"I blew it twenty-five years ago, Danny, and I want a second chance. Will you think about giving me one?"

I reached out and turned her face toward me.

We all want to know what happened to the First Great Love of our lives, but we never think about the danger in actually finding out. Meet someone after half a lifetime, someone who was once the center of your world, and you risk seeing all the signs of diminished hope or smashed dreams embedded in their face like scars, or – worse – discovering that they've gone on to be happy without you. I used to fantasize about a moment when Laura Kirwan would return, a broken shell of the girl I once knew, and beg me – Mr. Astronaut/Rock Star/Famous Author/World-Renowned Physicist to take her back.

Arrogant male bullshit, that; I know.

I hadn't made it and neither had she, not in the ways we'd imagined at seventeen, but you'd never be able to tell it from her face; it was older, yes, a few more lines here and there, crows' feet when she smiled, but aside from these inevitable tracks of time's forward march, she was no less beautiful in my eyes now than she'd been in high school. In fact, if anything, age had given her humility and grace and made her all the more stunning.

"We can talk about this later," I said. "You're welcomed to stay here with Blair and me as long as you want, until you figure out what you need to do."

"I knew that's what you'd say."

"I'm still that predictable?"

"No," she said, squeezing my hand. "You're dependable. You're loyal and true."

"You make me sound like Dudley Do-Right."

"Dudley's gonna be on soon," said Blair. I blinked – I'd almost forgotten she was in the kitchen with us.

Laura saved the day: *"Really?"*

"Uh-huh."

"I *love* Dudley!"

Blair grinned. "'I save you, Nell.'"

"Can I watch Dudley with you?"

Blair's face lit up. "Oh, yes!" And she left to tune in the Dudley Channel.

Laura smiled after her, then looked at me. "How long have you been caring for her?"

"Since about a year before Mom died."

"Is that why you never. . . ?" She didn't have to finish the question.

"Yeah," I whispered.

We looked at each other.

Live your life as if you were already living for the second time and as if you had acted the first time as wrongly as you are about to act now.

I was getting ready to say something tender and profound, something that would have won the heart of any woman, something that would have gone down in the record books as the Most Brilliantly Poetic and Romantic Reply Ever, when there was a knock on the front door.

I looked up at the wall clock and saw that it was ten a.m.

Already I was so exhausted I was ready to pack in it, and it wasn't even noon yet.

"Shit," I whispered.

"You sweet talker."

"No – sorry, that wasn't for you. I forgot I was supposed to do something at ten." I leaned down and gave her a quick kiss on the lips. "This'll only take a minute. Go watch Dudley and Nell."

"Actually, I always thought Snidely Whiplash was pretty hot."

"I can't tell you how warm and fuzzy that makes me feel."

Out on the front porch, I found Mr. Finney waiting for me.

"Sorry it ain't the curb, but I waited almost five minutes."

"I apologize. I lost track of time."

"It's gone."

"*What?*"

"Take a look for yourself."

He was right. The streak of old white paint was gone. The front porch was once again uniform in color. We both touched the area where the streak had been, and found that the paint there was dry.

"Danny, does this seem odd to you?'

"It's actually a little scary, Mr. Finney."

"Do you believe in ghosts, Danny?"

"Why?"

"Do you think it's possible for a house to haunt itself?"

I thought about this for a moment.

"Mr. Finney, if you mean do I believe in the kind of ghosts that rattle chains and moan and make things go bump in the night, then, no, I don't. But I *do* believe in ghosts, sir. Quantum ones. Black holes and Special Relativity and Planck Time and how they make origami out of the sheeted layers of the universe." I glanced at him. He was looking at me as if I'd just told him I was an alien from the planet BoogerFart here to scout good locations for our upcoming Special Olympics.

"What I mean, Mr. Finney, is that less than two hours ago we both saw a section of this front porch as it was *before* I painted the house, and fifteen years ago, you and my father saw a section of fresh grey paint – *this paint* – in the same spot. There were no practical jokers, Mr. Finney. No one's touched this house except me. I painted it last year, and through some mix-up in the structure of time, a portion of this paint appeared on the porch fifteen years ago."

Finney shook his head. "I swear, the older I get and the more I learn, the less I think I know. How . . . how is something like that possible, Danny?"

"Why do you care about it in the first place?"

His eyes misted for a moment. "Because if what you said is true, then it means there's really forces beyond what we understand, and *that* means there's something more after this here life, and that means my Ethel'll be there waiting for me. I'll . . ." A tear crept to the corner of his eye. " . . . I'll see her again. Hold her again. My favorite and only girl. She won't be lonely anymore."

At that moment, I think I loved Mr. Finney as much as I'd loved my own father. Leave it to a man this genuinely decent to think only of his wife's loneliness, even years after her death.

I put a hand on his shoulder. "Maybe the universe is trying to tell us both something with all of this."

He took a handkerchief from his pocket and wiped his eye, then blew his nose. "I hope so, Danny. I truly do hope so." He smiled at me. "Sure would appreciate it if you'd come over for some lemonade soon. Bring Blair along, too."

"How's tomorrow? We'll bring lunch."

His smile widened and brightened. "That would be just great. Just great. I'll look forward to it."

I watched him walk back to his house, and hoped that it would seem a little less empty.

The universe is a four dimensional/four layered sheet; three existing in space, one in time.

The soul – be it of a person, place, or event – does not exist in space. 1.62 x 10^{33} is a smokescreen. Yes, time and space come apart at that point, and there are spaces between the layers, but only the soul, like images and words erased from a sheet of parchment, can make a physical impression on/in time.

And if the impression/perception is strong enough, if the past is more alive to the perceiver than the moment in which they exist now, then it matters not a damn if time came before space or vice-versa, because the soul takes control, and bleeds through the layers, and brings back What Was.

And, sometimes, if the need is great enough, it brings What Could Have Been.

6. Living in the Past/Love Reign O'er Me

That night I lay wide awake in my bed, thinking about how the rest of the day had gone while the clock-radio was tuned to an oldies station. Tonight seemed to be Sad Songs Night; "All By Myself" had just finished (mawkish piece of shit still managed to choke me up) and Don McLean's "Vincent" was just starting.

Blair and Laura got along wonderfully. They watched cartoons, made lunch, drew pictures (giving me a chance to explain the palimpsest effect, to their rapt, glassy-eyed boredom), then tried to teach me how to dance, soundtrack provided by two 70s favorites, "Life Is a Rock (But the Radio Rolled Me)" and "Get Down Tonight." How a K.C. and the Sunshine Band record *ever* got into my house is beyond me.

But underneath everything, I could sense an unease in Laura, a forced cheerfulness whenever she was around Blair. I was trying to figure out why when two things happened simultaneously: my bedroom door opened and the night light in the hallway flickered and went out. I knew I should have changed the bulb this morning, but the day had brought with it too many distractions.

"Danny?" It was Laura.

I sat up in bed, pulling on a t-shirt I grabbed from the floor. "You okay?"

"I'm fine," she whispered, and softly walked over to the bed. "Can I sit down beside you?"

"I, uh . . ."

She smacked my arm affectionately. "Don't flatter yourself, Studley. I didn't come up here because the call of your man-meat is irresistible. I was lonely down on the couch. I was just wondering if . . . if we could just lay next to each other and hold hands."

I moved over and patted the bed. She lay down next to me and we held hands.

"Danny?"

"Yeah?"

"I'm gonna tell you something, and I'd really appreciate it if you wouldn't look at me while I'm saying it, okay?"

"Okay."

"I really like Blair, I think she's sweet, and I am in awe of you having sacrificed so much to take care of her. It makes me realize all the more just how much I love you and what I've missed out on these last twenty-five years. I'm gonna move back here to Cedar Hill."

Listen to the thudding of my heart as she said this.

"But I can't . . . I can't help you care for her, Danny. I hope that doesn't make me an awful person in your eyes. I mean, maybe someday, later on, when I feel more comfortable being around someone like her – oh, God, that sounded rotten, didn't it? 'Someone like her.' I'm sorry."

"Don't worry about it."

"Do you hate me?"

"No."

At that moment, I hated just about everything else,

though. So the love of my life was coming back after all, to start her life over . . . and it would be without me. Oh, I knew she'd spend a lot of time with Blair and me at first, but after a while, she'd come around less and less, until, finally, her presence in my life would be reduced to a few phone calls . . . and even those would eventually stop. It was the pattern. In the years I'd been caring for Blair, I'd had only a handful of relationships with women, none of them going very deep or lasting very long because they couldn't handle being around ' . . . someone like her.'

I couldn't blame them. I couldn't blame Laura.

"It's always been you," I said to her.

"I know."

"Did you ever look at it? That picture I took of you that night?"

She laughed. "Oh, yeah."

"And. . . ?"

"And I look like a teen-aged girl who'd just gotten a really good fuck."

"How romantic."

"Tell me about it."

I felt a tear slip from the corner of my eye, run down my temple, and drip into my ear. "I wish things were different."

Laura squeezed my hand. "Me, too." Then: "You wouldn't ever consider . . . don't yell at me, okay?" She rose up on an elbow and rolled toward me, wiping the tear-streak from my skin. "Would you consider something like a group home for Blair? If you haven't done it because it's a money problem, I've got plenty, believe me. I'd pay for it."

"I promised Mom I wouldn't do that."

"Not to sound like a bitch, but your Mom's been dead for fifteen years."

"Thirteen-and-a-half," I said.

"Whatever. The point is, as much as I admire you for keeping your promise, don't you think it's time to start living the life you *should've* had?"

"Don't go there."

"Why not?"

"Because I can't start thinking about what *should have* been. Too many detours through depression and self-pity along that road."

And wouldn't you know it – right then the radio station started playing Roger Daltrey's "Oceans Away," a song that rips me to pieces every time.

I rolled away from Laura and looked into the darkness.

A few moments later, just when I was on the verge of really losing it because of that fucking song, I heard Blair bumping around in the hallway.

"Damn it," I said.

"What is it?"

"Blair. She doesn't see very well in the dark, that's why I've got a night light out there. She's trying to find the bathroom." I started to get out of bed. Laura put a hand on my arm.

"You stay here, Danny. I'll go."

She quietly left the room. I suspected that once she'd helped Blair get to and from the bathroom, she wouldn't come back.

The song finished and I turned the radio off before they played "Shannon" or something even worse, and that's when I heard it.

The sound of someone coming *up* the stairs.

Blair's room and the bathroom were in the center of the hall, away from the stairs. I waited to see if Laura was going to surprise me and come back, and when she didn't step through the door again the old urban panic reared its irrational head.

Someone had broken into the house.

I slowly got up and crouched down to retrieve the baseball bat I keep under the bed – my one compromise in this age of ever-deadly home security. I'd never keep a gun in the house, but a ball bat . . . oh, yeah.

I got a good grip on it and crept toward the door.

It was only as I was stepping into the hall that I realized the floor under my bare feet felt fuzzy. I looked down.

Carpeting. Shag carpeting.

From one end of the hall to the other.

I looked around, stepped fully into the hall, and started toward Blair's room. I was almost there when I heard someone behind me.

I whirled around and saw the intruder at the top of the stairs.

I pulled back my arms, readying the bat, and started moving toward them, so filled with panic that I didn't bother to register what they looked like, only that it was neither Blair nor Laura, and I was all set to knock their legs out from under them – was just starting to get my swing going – when the night light flickered and I saw my mother.

My mother as she'd looked in 1974.

Before there was a Blair.

I stood there, the bat cocked at my shoulder, and watched her slip her foot under the piece of loose carpeting on the landing.

She rehearsed it once, then once again.

It was the interval between the second rehearsal and her actual attempt that the impressions previously erased joined with new ink and began to bleed through for me:

. . . Live your life as if you were already living for the second time and as if you had acted the first time as wrongly as you are about to act now . . .

. . . at 1.62 x 10^{33} *space and time come apart . . .*

. . . and this sheet of parchment upon which I had drawn my new life was giving way to the lives and memories drawn in this space before . . .

. . . "Thas' Mommy's candy. Gonna get it if you eat any" . . .

. . . "Because if what you said is true, then it means there's really forces beyond what we understand, and that means there's something more after this here life, and that means my Ethel'll be there waiting for me" . . .

. . . "I mean, maybe someday, later on, when I feel more comfortable being around someone like her" . . .

. . . and Mom started moving toward the top of the stairs.

I knew that the "breeze" she'd felt that night was me swinging the bat at someone I thought was an intruder.

She was gaining speed. When her foot hit that carpeting, she'd go down hard. Not hard enough to kill her, but it would be enough to make her lose the baby that only she and the doctor knew she was carrying.

I suddenly saw What Might Have Been become What *Can* Be.

I saw a future with Laura and a new past where my youth was mine and all potentials had been explored and realized.

I saw a life without constant worry, without daily arguments, without Blair screaming and saying that she hated me, without tantrums that left me with bloody noses and spit on the floor and used tampons thrown at me.

All I had to do was just stand here and *not* swing the bat.

Mom breezed past me.

The night light flickered again, then came all the way on –

– Mom seemed to notice that from the corner of her eye –

– and all I had to do to claim the life that should have been mine . . . was nothing.

Nothing at all.

Mom's foot caught under the piece of carpeting. . . .

7. Lucky Man

I saw a kid today who was wearing bell-bottom jeans and a buckskin jacket with a Smiley Face sewn onto its back, the words "Have A Nice Day" painted in Day-Glo colors underneath it.

As he approached, I couldn't help but look down at his left hand and, sure enough, he was wearing a Mood Ring that shone a deep azure-blue. I wondered if he'd gotten these antiques from a parent, an aunt or uncle, or if he'd shelled out a good portion of his savings account to purchase all this stuff at one of the retro shops that have been multiplying like bacteria since the middle of the 90s. I stared in a combination of awe and embarrassment; my God, did we really look that absurd back then? Someone should have said something – we thought we looked *good.*

The kid caught me staring at him and up came his middle and index fingers in the "peace" sign. I couldn't help what I did next; I smiled at him and returned the gesture.

"Outta sight man," he said on his way past. "Groovy. Far Out."

"Keep on truckin'," I replied.

"Huh?"

I whispered the next as if it was some kind of secret code: *"Dave's not here, man."*

For a second, those words managed to stop him in his tracks (obviously he'd never been exposed to the pot-haze whimsy of Cheech & Chong); if he said anything to me after that, I'll never know: I was distracted by a voice calling, "Danny! Wait up!"

I turned and waited for her to catch up with me.

I smiled as the girl I loved more than anything in the world came up and took hold of my hand.

"I thought you hated it when I held your hand like this."

"Nah," said Blair. "I like it." She playfully bumped her shoulder against mine. "I like having you for a brother."

"That's sweet . . . but I'm still not buying you roller blades."

"Thas' okay. Where we goin' today?"

"That's up to you. It's your birthday."

"Wanna go see Laura?"

"No, we didn't call. We always call first. She has a husband and kids, you know. We can't just show up like we used to."

"I know. I just . . . miss her sometimes."

"Me too. But, hey, *we* have fun, right?"

"We have *all* the fun."

"So what do you want to do?"

"Go to the bookstore an' then have some lemonade with Mr. Finney?"

"Mr. Finney died last month, Blair. Remember we went to the funeral?"

"Oh. . . ." She looked as if she were going to cry.

"But he had a good life. He's happy now. He's with his wife."

"Thas' good."

I squeezed her hand. "So, you want to go to your big

brother's bookstore, huh?"

"Yes. When we get home, can we have some of that chocolate cake I found?"

"You mean the one from the Birthday Cake Fairy? You bet."

And off we went, returning to the life I'd almost been stupid and selfish enough to throw away.

There was a time when Ayds (spelled with a "y") was a popular and surprisingly tasty dietetic candy that came in plastic bags containing individually-wrapped pieces. You could easily find it on store shelves right alongside Sweathog coffee mugs, *The Wit and Wisdom of Archie Bunker,* Kiss comic books, and *Chico and the Man* lunch boxes. There was a time when a nerdy kid at Cedar Hill High School dreamed of being an astronaut or rock star, maybe a famous author or great scientist – but whatever he became, he'd be married to the cheerleader he was in love with.

There was a time when he looked at his new baby sister and wondered why her face was so weird.

There was a time when the past seemed more real and desirable to him because he couldn't stop looking behind him . . . until he stepped out into a dark hallway one night and realized that all he'd wanted from life was someone to love him unconditionally for as long as he lived, and that he'd been so busy looking back he never realized that that someone had been with him all along.

I let go of Blair's hand and told her it was okay for her to walk on ahead.

She waited at the light until it changed and the WALK signal shone. She crossed the street then turned and waved at me. She smiled, so very pleased with having finally crossed a street on her own.

I smiled and waved back, twice as proud of her as she was of herself.

When I joined her, she took my hand and led me forward, slowly, with great dignity.

Then I sneezed.

"Kahoutek," she said.

"Foghat," I replied.

"Huh?"

www.ingramcontent.com/pod-product-compliance
Lightning Source LLC
Chambersburg PA
CBHW020614310726
48979CB00008B/1479/J

* 9 7 8 1 5 9 2 2 4 5 9 7 0 *